THE FIRST SISTER

DANIELLE LEUKAM

A DANGEROUS BLOODLINE

BY DANIELLE LOUISE LEUKAM

Editor: Christine Weimer with Our Galaxy Publishing - https://ourgalaxypublishing.com/
Blurb: Christine Weimer with Our Galaxy Publishing - https://ourgalaxypublishing.com/
Formatting: Briggs Consulting, LLC - https://amybriggsauthor.com/
Secondary Editor: Cassey Bailey
Cover Design by: Med City Creative - https://www.medcitycreative.com
Cover Photographer: Twelve Ten Photography – https://www.1210.photography

www.facebook.com/daniellelouiseleukam
www.instagram.com/danielleleukam
www.twitter.com/danielle_leukam
www.patreon.com/danielleleukam

Sponsored by:
The Boutique Station and Stanger Construction

Trigger Warning: This is a fictional thriller. This book contains graphic descriptions of sexual assault, childhood sexual assault, and breast cancer.

1
_____

11:47 p.m.

Blood dripped to the floor like a leaky faucet, creating a pool of red on the tile in a matter of seconds. The gash on her hand was deep; the knife went through her flesh and into her muscle, nearing the bones. She sat on the floor of the bathroom against the tub with only her shirt on, her body trembling uncontrollably as tears slid down her face. She was speechless, as though staying quiet would save her, but she knew she was running out of options.

Less than ten minutes prior, the door to her bedroom had been shut as it was every other night. The handle was old and worn, and it was nearly impossible to open the door silently. That's how she woke up. The sound of the handle turning filled the quiet air, waking her instantly. Her green eyes shot open, and she was suddenly wide awake, yet motionless, as she tried to process what she heard. *My husband couldn't possibly be home,* she thought. A second later, her bedroom door flew open, and a man stormed in, leaping straight for her, landing heavily on the bed. His landing knocked the bedside lamp off her nightstand; its shatter ripping through the once peaceful night. She couldn't help but scream while kicking her legs, trying to sit up quickly to be in a better position to fight or to run.

"No!" she yelled as she felt his hand close down around her leg to pull her toward him. Once he was close enough, he used his weight to pin her in place. She kicked and thrashed as she tried to free herself from the stranger's grip. Realizing she wouldn't give up, he finally asked, "Do you want to die?" He gave her a moment to answer. When she didn't, he threatened, "I'll kill you if you keep fighting! I will kill you."

"Please don't hurt me. Please. Take whatever you want," she offered, her voice trembling and her body growing hot and wet with sweat.

In the glow of the nightlight plugged in near the bathroom, she caught a glimpse of his wild, dark eyes as he continued to hold her down on the bed that she was sleeping so peacefully in just a moment before. It was the gruff, demanding, harsh tone of his voice, his aggressive motions, and the sweat seeping through his shirt that made her realize his need to be in control. His breath was hot and smelled of decay, as though he'd never been to a dentist. She did not recognize this man's voice. *Who is he? Why is he here? What did I do to deserve this? Why me?*

"Don't move," he demanded, peering down at her.

She complied, appeasing the stranger in front of her. She noticed he was of average height but moved fluidly as though he'd done this before. His strength and agility frightened her as he held her in place while tearing off her silk night-shorts. Every move he made reiterated the lack of control she possessed. She no longer consciously had to think about *not* fighting him, she had simply stopped. The threats against her caused her to become limp. She realized she needed to continue to appease him while coming up with a plan for escape. Warm, salty tears streamed down her face, prompted by her helplessness, loss of worth, and strong desire to stay alive. All she wanted was to wake up from her nightmare to realize none of it was real. But the feeling of her stomach sinking to the floor, and the ache of her heart as she thought of her son, reminded her that she was indeed awake.

Just when she wondered what he would do to her, he flipped her from her back onto her stomach. In this position, he used his knees to separate her legs, exposing her bottom. She felt his right-hand lift, yet she was still held in place by his left hand and the weight of his upper body pushing down on her. Even as her sheets surrounded her face, she could still smell his strong and repulsive body odor.

He lowered himself between her legs and forcefully pushed into her. He was hard, as though her hysteria beneath him only made him more aroused. She detached from her body as he raped her, lying there like an emotional, defenseless rag doll, losing all sense of worth. She was defeated and under his complete control.

His stench filled her nostrils, making her nauseous as he slowed his motions, grunting as he finished inside of her. She felt his heavy weight relax on top of her back as he lay down. He was throbbing inside of her, breathing heavily into her hair. Her breaths became shallow as his weight crushed her, causing her anxiety to heighten.

"I can't breathe. I can't breathe," she cried. But he stayed on top of her, unmoving, trying to catch his breath.

When she felt her head become foggy from the lack of

oxygen, the weight was released from her back, and he removed himself from inside of her. She waited for him to say something, do something, or leave her bedroom. Instead, he flipped her over onto her back, repositioning himself on top of her, straddling her before putting a knife to her throat.

"Please, please don't. I have a son, a husband. They'll be home soon. Please!" she begged. She wanted nothing more than to live. She wanted to see her son again and be held in her husband's strong and safe arms. She wanted to breathe the fresh air of freedom and feel the warm sun tan her face. She wanted to sit on her front porch watching her son play basketball in the driveway. But she knew he had no reason to let her live, so her fear of death caused a sudden adrenaline rush to overpower her submission.

But instead of leaving, he laughed. Anger took over, and her mind became clear as it came back in touch with her body, and she took advantage of that sudden burst of energy. She screamed with her jaw clenched as she pushed the knife away from her neck. The blade sliced her palm, causing her jaw to unclench and her scream to become louder. The man was low enough on her body that when her knees came up, she was able to use her legs to kick him off like a jackrabbit. He landed hard on the floor in front of the door and smashed his head against the dresser. The man slowly got himself on all fours, moaning and swaying back and forth when she realized the door he landed near was her exit. That beautiful wooden door with the squeaky knob led to the hallway that led to the kitchen that would eventually lead her outside to freedom. Too afraid to go near the man to get to the door, she instead ran to the bathroom before he got himself back on his feet.

"Fuck! You bitch!" she heard him yell as she slammed the bathroom door shut behind her.

She clicked the door lock and gasped for air. She leaned back against the wall, struggling to breathe as though his weight was still on top of her crushing her lungs. The wall was smooth as she slid to the floor, anticipating the door breaking open any second.

Her eyes were wide, and her heart was beating hard inside her chest wall as she frantically looked around for anything she could use as a weapon. Surely the old lock on the ten-dollar doorknob wasn't going to hold him out for long. Her eyes darted around the small room, catching the shine from the silver bar near the shower.

The towel bar.

The bathroom door handle jiggled as she stood and tore the bar off the wall, holding it like a bat. He kicked open the locked door and said, "You should have just been a good girl," before charging toward her.

"You asshole!" she screamed as she swung hard at him, but she was not quick enough. He blocked the towel bar with his left arm and tackled her into the bathtub, smashing her head against the tile wall. Her hand tried to grip the wall as she went down, leaving behind a streak of crimson blood.

"Help! Please, stop!" she screamed, despite knowing there was no one else in the house to hear her cries. His hands went around her throat, pressing down and squeezing at the same time. Now unable to speak, she wished she could do anything to remind him that she was a mom, a wife, a friend, a human and not an object.

Please, please, stop. I'll give you anything you want, she wanted to say, but she was pinned to the bottom of the tub, unable to throw his heavy weight off again. But she saw no remorse or sympathy in his eyes, only cold darkness.

Her anxiety was waning as her oxygen levels depleted. Her eyes widened as she thrashed around as much as she could, but soon her fight weakened, and her grip on his shirt released as the lights faded. Soon, everything went black.

2

Sunday, June 20, 2021

9:35 a.m.

"Nine-one-one, what is your emergency?"

"Please! Send help! Please! My wife isn't breathing! She isn't moving! I think she's dead! There's...there's blood everywhere! Stacie! Honey, please!"

3

SUNDAY, JUNE 20, 2021

6:00 p.m.

"Hello. I'm Tracy Johnson reporting live from 708 Walnut Avenue here in Winona. Police say they found a woman's body in the bathtub of her home around 11:30 this morning. She was reportedly found by her husband and young son, who were away for the weekend. There are no other victims and no suspects at this time. Police are actively investigating the crime scene, hoping to find the person who committed this heinous act."

DEPUTY ZANQUINNETTE RAMIRO and Deputy Douglas McGriff were at the home less than five minutes after the call came through from dispatch. Zan's ebony skin was flawless. She was naturally beautiful, radiating in anything she wore—even her police uniform. Douglas was quite the opposite; a heavier man but one of the stronger ones in the department. As they pulled up, Zan saw that the woman's husband and son were waiting out on the front lawn, sobbing in an embrace.

"Sir, I'm Deputy Zan Ramiro, and this is Deputy Douglas McGriff. Can you tell me, is there anyone else inside the house?" Zan asked the woman's husband.

He wiped his nose with the back of his hand, looked up at her, and said, "No, not that I know of. Just my wife, Stacie." The man hugged his son tighter and looked away from Zan as though he had nothing more to say.

"Okay, sir. I'm going to go into your home, okay?" Zan asked. The man didn't look at her, but he nodded his consent.

She led the way up the steps of the home with her right hand on her gun, pushing the door open with her left hand as she stepped inside. McGriff was only two steps behind. "Hello?" Ramiro called out. There was no response.

Ramiro and McGriff stayed close but kept an eye out in opposite directions. The large family photo above the fireplace caught their attention. Everything on the main level was immaculate, including the image of the family who had lived there. Nothing downstairs had been touched. It was as though the intruder was truly after only one thing. The victim.

After determining the main level was all clear, they made their way upstairs to where they were told the woman was. Ramiro grabbed her radio, held it to her lips, and said, "All clear on the main level," to the crew on the ground.

"Jesus," McGriff said as he approached the tub, noticing Stacie's pale body lying at the bottom with her legs bent at an abnormal angle. They were careful not to step on or touch anything that could have been considered evidence.

"This was not an accident," Ramiro determined as she noticed the blood on the bathroom floor, shower wall, and the markings around the woman's neck. She crouched down to get a closer look at the bathtub, looking for any additional clues. As she looked at the blood smeared on the wall of the shower, she tried to envision how everything from the night prior had unfolded.

McGriff grabbed his radio and said, "Create a perimeter. This entire house is a crime scene."

HOURS LATER, reporters surrounded the home and tensions were high. Caution tape had been placed around the house, keeping news crews and neighbors at a distance. By this time, the Bureau of Criminal Apprehension (BCA) had arrived.

"It's apparent there was a struggle in both the bedroom and bathroom," Zan noted.

"The investigators found fingerprints on the bathroom doorknob. But they're unsure if the prints are the murderer's, the victim's, or the husband's," McGriff said.

Douglas McGriff was Zan's partner; they were opposite in some ways but similar in their work habits, making them the perfect team. They made the same judgment calls and proved to be excellent at having each other's back.

This became clear two years ago when McGriff had a bad gut feeling about a house call Zan was going to solo. Not being able to shake that something felt off, McGriff showed up at the house a few minutes after Zan arrived. By this time, a gun had been pulled on Zan and she found herself in a standoff with the man accused of domestic assault. The situation was quickly controlled after McGriff pulled his gun, leaving two loaded guns aimed at the perpetrator, and what they would soon find out, one unloaded Glock pointed at Zan. Realizing he was outnumbered with no way out, the man lowered his weapon and willingly went with Zan to the squad car in handcuffs.

The two had multiple gut feelings about situations during the course of their time as partners, saving each other from danger each time. It was almost as though they were twins and were able to sense when the other was in trouble.

"Let me know when you run them through the system," Ramiro said to some of the other investigators. "I want to know if those prints match with anyone. This guy is going to be behind bars for a long, long time." There was a deep anger in her voice as she spoke. She turned and stormed out of the bathroom, knocking over a plastic vase with fake flowers in it as she descended the stairs. She gave no opportunity for anyone to reply. She had an excellent track record at the Winona County Police Department. While she was no longer an investigator herself, she quickly and efficiently solved numerous crimes, putting away child molesters, drug dealers, and domestic abusers. A murder in her county was *not* going to go unsolved.

McGriff was left upstairs, watching Ramiro storm away, knowing she would be vested in this case. She was known for empowering women and advocating for women's rights. Seeing a woman murdered in her own home was not going to be easy for Zan to step away from.

"Yeah, if we catch the son-of-a-bitch," McGriff said, replying to Ramiro even though she was long gone.

Ramiro was getting a brief report from one of the deputies that spoke with the woman's husband. He finished by saying, "Stacie was a yoga instructor. My fiancé went to her class every Saturday. She always loved her. I feel bad for her husband and kiddo. The kid was so hysterical we almost couldn't get him off the front lawn. He's going to be traumatized from this, that's for sure."

"Thanks, Joe," Ramiro said as she noticed McGriff coming down the front porch steps.

She nodded to McGriff as though she were asking, "What's up?"

"We found something interesting in the tub after they moved the body," McGriff stated.

"Yeah?" she asked.

"There was a white rose petal next to Stacie's face. She doesn't have any roses in the house. It's probably a fluke, but who knows. We're keeping it as evidence," McGriff said.

4

7:42 a.m.

Dew on the grass glistened in the light of the early morning sun as Kate Sampson locked her front door on her way out of the house. The birds were chirping, the clouds were sparse, and it was going to be a beautiful day despite the high humidity. Her long brown hair was in a bun to save herself from looking like a frizzy mess halfway through the day. Her petite frame fit well into summer dresses, a style she grew up loving because of her mom. Kate's soft but mesmerizing features turned heads everywhere she went.

After three steps down the porch from her gray two-story home, and onto her sidewalk that led to the road, Kate took the short walk to the store she owned called Julie's. She passed a realtor removing the "sold" sign from the house next door on her way. It was a simple white rambler-style house that desperately needed some work done. The white siding was so dirty it almost looked tan, the shutters were mismatched, and the last time Kate went into the house, she quickly learned that the carpets had never been washed or replaced. The new neighbor had already started to move in last week, but she still hadn't met him yet. Supposedly he was from the next town over, looking for a fresh start.

She headed north and passed a huge brick house her high school friend had grown up in and another house that was engulfed in trees, shrubs, and tall grass. Only one more block north led her straight to what was formerly her mother Julie's store, her place of Zen. She stood out front for a moment, admiring the store's facade and the lilies blooming in the landscape. Kate and her mom planted the lilies years ago on her birthday, and each year they returned more beautiful than the last. The four walls of the one-story vintage brick building surrounded her with vivid memories of her mother. It was only ten feet from the neighboring structure to the north, the hair salon. Kate knew the building that housed Julie's inside and out. Every nook and cranny and every crack and paint chip were on a list for her to fix.

Kate unlocked the front door and made her way inside, reenacting the daily routine she'd grown to maneuver through as second nature. She turned on the open sign that hung in the front window before making her way to the back room, where she stored her purse in her locker. The Keurig in the back was a lifesaver. She turned it on and went out to the register while the water heated.

JULIE'S HAD a bit of everything. There was a hardware section for at-home projects, snacks and candy, birthday cards, medical supplies, hygiene products, books, and more. Every year, Kate grew to learn what customers in town needed, and she supplied everything in demand. Julie wanted her store to be a go-to place for everyone in town since the two nearest cities with the shopping malls and grocery stores were so far away.

Four hours at the store flew by. She only realized the time because the bells above the door sounded as Ashley came inside to start her shift.

"Hey, Kate," she said with a smile, her boyfriend Alex following close behind. *She really needs to get her car back from the shop,* Kate thought to herself, noticing Alex had been driving her everywhere she went. Alex and Ashley had been dating for a few weeks now, and she seemed to be head over heels for him and his free spirit. Ashley's smile revealed her perfectly white teeth that paired so well with her long blonde hair. She was thirty years old and had been working for Kate for over twelve years. She started working evenings and weekends while she finished high school, then began working longer hours after graduation as she tried to figure out where she wanted her life to go. Years later, she still hadn't figured out anything other than being at Julie's. Kate was thankful to have Ashley, though. She trusted her and could focus on bookkeeping and remodeling the store leaving customer service in Ashley's hands.

Kate's other hired help was Nancy, the nicest woman in all of southeast Minnesota. She'd been working there since the beginning when Kate's mom, Julie, opened the store. Now Nancy only worked four days a week, but she reminded Kate of her mother and memories of them working together while she was growing up. Nancy's love for Kate and the store was apparent, and Kate was grateful she was still willing to work with her.

"Hey, Ashley. How was the weekend?" Kate asked.

"Oh my God! It was amazing. I never thought they would come back to Minnesota, but I'm *so* glad they did,"

Ashley said, referring to her favorite podcast hosts, two female comedians who talk about true crime.

"It was seriously amazing," Ashley continued.

"You should have come with us," Alex added.

"And be the third wheel on your date?" Kate replied, glancing at Alex. "Nope."

"Oh whatever," Ashley said as she and Alex headed toward the back room to the lockers where she would punch in with her timecard. "You never go out. I think you need to broaden your horizons and scope out potential boyfriend candidates."

Kate leaned over the register, reaching to the front of the counter to straighten the books on display, laughing as though Ashley had made a joke. The doorbells chimed, and Kate stood up, smiled, and greeted her customer.

"Hey there," Kate said, acknowledging him. It had been a challenge recognizing everyone by just seeing their eyes when masks were mandated because of COVID-19, but even with the mandate lifted and seeing the customer's full face, she did not recognize him.

"Hi," he replied with a generous smile, but that's all he offered. He went on with his business, looking around as though on a mission for something in particular.

Kate went to stock the shelves near the register, adding Fourth of July decorations. The man quietly came to the bookshelf at the front of the store. She noticed his dirty jeans with holes in them as he browsed the shelves. His neon orange shoes caught her eye. He'd already grabbed what he came for; electrical tape and outlet covers. He was a good-looking guy with a small scar above his right eyebrow that caught her attention, just below his thick, dark hair styled with gel. He had a strong jawline that wasn't clean-shaven but only had a couple of days of beard stubble. She couldn't help but notice his thick and worn hands as though he'd been working a laborious job and his large forearms that showed all of his veins as though he'd just finished a weight-lifting workout. She saw the bottom of a tattoo under the sleeve of his t-shirt but couldn't quite make out what it was. *A cat?*

He pulled a best-selling book off the shelf about a shepherd boy who followed his heart and his omens. It was Kate's favorite book of all time, one that she'd read multiple times over the years. The man turned toward Kate, giving her a subtle smile while setting the book, electrical tape, and outlet covers on the counter. There was yellow tape on the ground in front of the cash register to mark where customers should stand to follow the COVID-19 six-foot social-distancing guidelines set by the Center for Disease Control.

"Did you find everything okay?" Kate asked.

"I did, yeah. Thank you," he offered.

"This is my favorite book," Kate said, scanning the barcode and placing it into a bag. "Once I opened the cover, I just couldn't put it down."

"Yeah, that happened to me, too. But I seemed to have lost my copy when I moved."

"Are you new to town?" she asked.

"Kind of. I'm from the area, just new to this particular town. I live in a house where the previous owners were terrible do-it-yourselfers. I'm surprised the place hasn't burned down already," he said, eyeing the electrical tape he bought.

She smiled as he handed her cash. She returned his change, her hand gently brushing his as she did.

"Good luck with the house," Kate added.

He quickly put the coins in his pocket and said, "Thank you, ma'am."

Such a respectful guy, she thought.

"See you again," she added. Most of her customers were kind, just like this one. But occasionally, she got the ones who rarely left their house, and when they did, they were grumpy as hell to see the light of day.

"Well, jeez, what did I miss?" Ashley asked with a grin after the man left the store. She and Alex saw their exchange of coins.

"Oh, stop!" Kate demanded of Ashley, giving her a giddy smile.

Alex leaned over to Ashley and kissed her on the cheek, "I'll pick you up at eight."

"Okay," Ashley said, smiling as though she were a middle-schooler. "See ya later, babe."

As Alex left the store, Kate turned to Ashley and asked, "Do you know who that guy is?" referring to customer who had just left.

"Nope. I've never seen him before. He was kind of cute though, don't ya think?" Ashley replied, winking at Kate.

"Yeah, in a shy way. But he reads. That's definitely a plus."

5

MONDAY, JUNE 21, 2021

7:50 p.m.

Finally catching up on monthly reports, Kate called it a day. She had taken over running Julie's when her mom was diagnosed with breast cancer. Julie had opened the store over thirty years ago when Kate was barely old enough to walk. The store was everything to her, second to Kate, of course. Her boyfriend at the time was a drunken drug addict, eventually showing the rage he initially hid so well from her. When they separated, Julie felt like she had been given a second chance at life, so she did what she'd always wanted to do. She was done being treated terribly by a man that didn't love her, and she was done working for her sleaze-ball boss, stuck in a tiny cubicle at a company that paid minimum wage. Instead, she took charge of her own life and became her own boss by opening a convenience store.

When Kate turned sixteen, she started working with her mom, stocking shelves and running the register as soon as school let out for the day. She'd often stay with her mom until closing time. They would quickly eat dinner in the backroom until they heard the bells on the front door when someone came in, taking turns going to the front to greet the customer.

On a cold day in 2019, Kate and her mom anxiously sat in a consult room at the number one clinic in the nation after a week of various appointments and tests. A doctor came into the room with a somber look on his face. "Julie, the results of your biopsy have come back showing malignancy." The lump she found on her breast was cancer. The doctor presented all options for treating the cancer, and they decided together she would undergo chemotherapy, then surgery.

Kate held her mom's hand tight after they left the clinic. They were sitting in Julie's car when Kate said, "It's going to be okay, Mom. I'm going to go to every appointment with you. We're in this together." Sitting in the passenger's seat, Julie didn't reply, but rather stared straight ahead, blank-faced.

Kate knew she would be her mom's caretaker while also having to take care of the store. Stepping up for the job, she took her mom to all of her chemotherapy appointments. Every third Thursday at ten in the morning, they would park downtown Rochester and head to the tenth floor of the clinic. After hours of receiving the chemotherapy infusion, a dose of Zofran for nausea, and holding a sick bucket for when the Zofran wasn't enough, they'd head back to Dover where her mom could rest.

A couple of months after chemotherapy was completed, Julie underwent a double mastectomy. She recovered at home for six weeks while Kate ran the store with the help of Nancy and Ashley. She couldn't have done it without them. Going to appointments, taking care of her mom, and running the store alone would have been too much to bear.

Kate would do anything to keep Nancy and Ashley happy, feeling like she owed them the world. Julie helped as much as she could, mostly with ordering and bookkeeping. Kate realized it was helpful for Julie to feel productive and needed, so she would go to her for questions about the store despite already having the answers she needed from Nancy.

In September 2020, the cancer they thought was gone had metastasized, and soon enough, it was taking over Julie's body. Kate became angry; she couldn't lose her mom. She was angry at God, the world, and herself for feeling like she should have done more. It wasn't fair. Julie had done all the things she was supposed to do. She had chemotherapy, lost most of her hair, had surgery, and all of the follow-up appointments suggested by the oncologist. But only a few short months later, Julie passed away. It was the day after Christmas.

Kate sunk deep into depression and into work at the store. She redecorated, reorganized, and made all new marketing plans to keep her mind occupied. She was over-compensating for losing her mother, but the store looked better than it ever had before.

An American flag gently swayed in the breeze out front as Kate placed Fourth of July decorations in the entryway for the upcoming holiday. She felt accomplished upon locking the door at eight o'clock, covering the last fifteen minutes of the day for Ashley. Alex had come to pick her up a bit early. He occasionally waited in the store for her to finish up, but today he'd sat in his rusty old car waiting. Kate locked up and walked over to a bar called The Dugout across the street, where she met with one of her best friends, Deputy Zan Ramiro.

.   .   .

"I HAVE no idea what to get Amy for our anniversary. I mean, she's so hard to shop for," Zan said, referring to her wife, Amy. "I could get her flowers and take her to the Surly brewery, but is that enough?"

Hesitating for only a moment, Kate replied, "How about tickets to the Twins game this Saturday?"

"Yes! You're so smart. What would I do without you?" Zan replied.

"I don't know. You probably wouldn't be married, though!" she said. Kate and Amy had known each other since they were toddlers. Amy was the girl who tried to flush Barbie down the toilet at daycare while Kate guarded the door, watching for the daycare staff.

Zan had met Kate years ago when her store had been broken into. Kate called the police as soon as she saw the shattered glass of the front window scattered all over the pavement. As a new police deputy, Zan had responded and miraculously caught the thieves—two teenagers, high on marijuana, looking for munchies.

Kate introduced Zan and Amy at a festival in Rochester, and the three of them had become a trio of best friends. "And how about the Ellen DeGeneres book? Has she read that?" Kate asked.

"And she strikes again! Ladies and gentlemen! Kate Sampson over here! She's the real deal!" Zan yelled, not caring that there were a handful of other people drinking quietly in the bar.

"Knock it off, you fool!" Kate scolded.

Zan had to laugh, but a moment later, her face became somber. "But for real," Zan said, "Did you see the news about the lady who was murdered yesterday? Her husband found her dead in the bathtub."

"Yeah, I saw that. She was raped too, I heard," Kate replied. Having been sexually assaulted as a child, she was sensitive about the topic. She'd become hyper-aware of her surroundings and still struggled with PTSD and anxiety. "That's two rapes now this month. The first one wasn't murdered, though. Do you think it was the same guy?" Kate questioned, furrowing her brow at the thought.

"I don't know, but shit's getting real, and I'm getting a security system installed, that's for damn sure. I mean, Rocky is big and tough and all, but I don't know if his 50-pound hairy ass could scare off an intruder," Zan said, referring to her 10-month-old black lab. "You should too. Amy and I can help you put it in."

"I had considered it in the past, but now there's just no question about it," Kate replied. "What are the odds it was two different guys, though? I just have a feeling it's the same person. What if it keeps happening?"

"Okay, well, get out your damn phone and order Simpli-Safe, and as soon as you get it, we're coming over to help you." Zan and Amy lived on the south end of town, just a couple of minutes away from Kate. Amy, who was both brilliant and beautiful, worked twelve-hour shifts as a registered nurse in the local Emergency Room (ER). Occasionally Zan and Amy had to work with the same victims and criminals, but they were able to do so professionally and efficiently.

Kate could always count on them to help. She did almost everything independently as a single woman, homeowner, and store owner, but she found, for her sanity, that it didn't hurt to accept help once in a while.

After an hour of catching up, Zan dropped off Kate at

her two-story home lined with flower beds where a string of porch lights stayed on all year round, greeting her when she arrived home, glowing in the darkness of the small-town's starry night. Kate wished her new neighbor had done the same, but instead of turning on the lights as the previous owner did, he had taken them all down.

6
_____

The room was an awful sight. There were clothes strewn all over the floor, mixed in with wrappers from the fast food they'd eaten the night before. There were empty beer bottles and tipped-over glasses that once held whiskey but instead kept fruit flies and the stench of a crowded bar after 2:00 a.m.

Nathan peered through the door at his mom, Natalie, passed out on the couch. Her hair was in a tangled knot at the top of her head, and an oversized t-shirt and basketball shorts covered her thin body. She looked as though she had passed out sitting upright but had tipped over onto her side.

Nathan—Nate for short—was inside his bedroom, too afraid to leave it. He looked cautiously from his mom to the kitchen, then back to his mom. He wasn't sure he wanted to risk being in the way. *It's not worth it,* he thought, retreating into his bedroom and quietly closing the door.

It had been one of those days for him, knowing that staying hidden was better than not. Tomorrow he would be turning eight, and all he wanted was someone to wish him a happy birthday. Instead, he wasn't sure his mom would even remember.

Nate's mom worked at a bar in the evenings. Money was not consistent, neither was her attendance at work. She'd gotten into heroin a couple of years prior when Nate was only five years old. It was the tipping point in her drug use when things at home declined significantly. Nate would cover his mom up at night with the couch blanket, then head to the kitchen where he would pour himself cereal or pull the bread out of the pantry for a cheese sandwich.

Neglected, alone, and afraid, Nate sat in his room imagining a new life with a new family. He'd never met his biological dad since he passed away when Nate was an infant, and the man Natalie was with when Nate turned seven stuck around, unfortunately. His name was Chuck. He didn't like to see or hear Nate, and when he did, it usually resulted in name-calling, yelling, and demanding chores to be done for his mother. That kind of abuse by itself had only lasted for a short while. Soon it had become physical too.

Nate's mom didn't treat him all that bad, but she went along with Chuck, defending him more than her child. Doing so kept Chuck happy. Things got even more ugly when Chuck was mad.

The first time Natalie realized the anger Chuck was capable of was a few weeks after he moved into their trailer. They had gotten into an argument about the electricity bill. Natalie swore she had paid the bill, but the electric company had shut the power off, leaving them with no air-conditioning and a fridge of food that would surely spoil if they didn't get the power back on soon. He accused her of using the money for drugs and alcohol, but she defended herself, which only worsened the argument. After only a few minutes of bickering back and forth, their arguing intensified. Chuck's face reddened, and the vein on his forehead pulsed with rage. A moment later, a dirty plate in the sink shattered on the wall next to Natalie's head after Chuck threw it at her. Natalie quickly realized she was not safe and tried to break things off. But somehow, Chuck had sweet-talked her back to him, temporarily mending their relationship. He was a master manipulator and Natalie forgave him.

Nate tried to be a good boy, but even if he had gotten all of his chores done by the time Chuck got home, he'd be called out for something else. The best thing he could do was hide in his room, waiting for them to pass out. If Nate fell asleep, his hunger would wake him up at a safe time for him to go to the kitchen.

The only safe place Nate had in his home was his bedroom. It was the place he spent most of his time. Except his bedroom did not stay a safe place for long. On his birthday the next day, he did not get a cake from his mom or Chuck. In fact, he was locked in his bedroom by a lock on the outside of his door that Chuck had placed shortly after he moved in with Natalie. He convinced her it was in Nate's best interest, and it would teach him boundaries and respect.

He sat there writing in his journal and telling stories of his day out loud to no one, imagining that the dad he never met was there with him, the dad who died when Nate was only six months old. He fantasized that maybe his dad was still alive, out there in the world and trying to find him. If his dad was alive, Nate imagined he would be a king living in a castle with a white horse and a silver sword he could use to scare Chuck away. Nate even designated a spot on his bed that his dad could sleep in if he ever came to his rescue.

·   ·   ·

SNOWFALL IN MINNESOTA had reached a record high during Nate's first winter. His dad Joe was the lead bartender at a classy place in Rochester that was frequented by politicians, doctors, and law enforcement. Nate's dad had to work closing shifts a few times a week on a rotation, leaving him as the closer when a polar vortex hit Minnesota. Temperatures were negative twenty degrees Fahrenheit with negative forty-degree wind chills. The wind was blowing hard across the roads, causing black ice and hazardous driving conditions.

On Joe's way home from work at 12:30 a.m. one morning, he hit a patch of black ice as he rounded a corner only a few miles from the house. He lost control and slid off the road. The depth of the ditch caused the car to flip four times before finally landing in the deep snow.

Headlights from the car pointed away from the road where no one could see them. After seven hours of being stuck upside down in his car, he was found dead the next morning. A semi-truck driver passing by sat high enough in his rig that he could see the back end of Joe's car in the field of snow down in the ditch. Once paramedics and deputies arrived, the semi-truck driver had already discovered that it was too late.

Nate was only with his dad for the first six months of his life, so he never grew to know him. Nate often dreamt about what life *could have been* like if his dad were alive. But now, he dreamt about what life would be like if he ran away.

7

TUESDAY, JUNE 22, 2021

5:12 p.m.

The next afternoon, another man came into Julie's who Kate didn't recognize. Dover, Minnesota was booming, so it was not uncommon for her to see people she didn't know in her store. New houses were going up like crazy, and the market was getting more competitive. As the man waltzed into the store, Kate noticed he was tall, tan, and hard to look away from. He glowed with confidence and wore a dark suit with a white dress shirt, no tie, polished shoes, and Oakleys. The top button of his white dress shirt was undone, understandably so in the ninety-five-degree weather Minnesota summers rarely saw. Nancy had the day off work to visit her grandkids, so Kate was covering the store.

"Excuse me, ma'am. Do you happen to sell paint here?" the man asked as Kate was stocking the bookshelf.

"I sure do," she replied, leading him toward the left side of the store. "What are you looking to paint?" Kate tried to make conversation as they neared the color samples.

Kate glanced over her shoulder and saw his eyes subtly

and quickly follow her yellow sundress down her hips to her bare legs, then to her white flats, and back up. Kate noticed his dark eyes as he took off his sunglasses to assess the paint colors. As she was admiring him, she silently acknowledged the brick wall she built around herself when she was a little girl, the one that kept men at a safe distance.

"My bedroom could use a new coat of paint. I prefer not to have lavender walls," he stated.

"No?" Kate asked, teasing. "Here are my color samples. I can mix up a small can for you if you want to try some out."

Rather than responding, he stepped closer to Kate. It wasn't the six-foot social-distancing guidelines that gave her goosebumps, but simply the closeness of another man— something she was not used to. He looked into her eyes for just a moment, then reached around her back to pick out a color sample from the wall behind her. He was close enough that she smelled his cologne, appreciating his cleanliness but skeptical about how forward he was with her. He pulled a light gray color combination off the rack and asked, "What do you think about this?"

"Classic gray. You can't go wrong with that," she said, taking a step out of his way to distance herself. "Do you want me to mix up a sample?"

"Sure, I suppose I should make sure it matches the lavender drapes the last owners left for me," he said, eliciting a laugh out of Kate.

They made small talk while she mixed the sample. He was a businessman from out of town, temporarily relocated here for a job opportunity. She rang him up at the register and said, "Here ya go. Is there anything else you need?"

"That'll do for now. Thank you again, ma'am," he replied.

"Kate," she corrected. "My name is Kate."

Extending a hand, he replied with a wink, "Brian. I'll see ya around, Kate."

Still thinking about Brian and how forward and close to her he had gotten, Kate closed up shop. She flipped off the OPEN sign, closed the blinds, turned out the lights, and locked the door behind her.

She always walked quickly at night with her pocket knife in her right pocket, purposefully staying off her phone so she could be one-hundred percent aware of her surroundings. She always carried a fear in the back of her mind that she was being watched, followed, and hunted because of her childhood sexual abuse, so she went to great lengths to feel safe by carrying small weapons and always looking over her shoulder.

The glow of her porch lights greeted her as she arrived home. They were set on a timer to turn on at seven o'clock every night—it was another safety measure she set up to brighten the perimeter of her house because of her fear of darkness. While it was a bit early in the summer, the darkness would have already taken over the daylight by the store's closing time in the winter. Kate struggled with the key in her doorknob for a moment before making her way inside.

"Damn lock," she said to herself. Her door handle and deadbolt were so old that she had to position the key just right to get it to unlock. An alarm system with a keypad to unlock the deadbolt would surely fix the issue.

The sound of her keys landing on the decorative stand in her entryway was a familiar pleasantry. She left her shoes by the front door before she headed toward the kitchen, famished after not having eaten since breakfast. She wasn't much of a cook, but she knew how to warm up a cup of instant oatmeal to just the right temperature. A hint of honey, a couple of walnuts, and an apple on the side. This was a typical meal for Kate. *No one to cook for but myself. So, what's the point?* She rationalized.

She turned on Hulu and crawled into her chair with her dinner and a glass of red wine. *Station 19* and *Grey's Anatomy* had new episodes out she wanted to catch up on. A perfect way to end her evening.

HOURS LATER, Kate woke in the night to a tapping on her window. A storm had rolled in, and she saw flashes of lightning outside, followed by loud claps of thunder. *How have I been sleeping through this?* She thought, suddenly wide awake. It took her only a moment to realize the tapping wasn't tree branches hitting the side of her house in the wind. It was louder than that.

Tap, tap, tap, tap.

Kate's heart raced, and her body shook with fear. The alarm on her nightstand showed 2:13 a.m.

The rain came pouring down on her steel roof louder than ever. When lightning struck again, a flash beamed through her window. In the sudden burst of light, Kate saw a man standing on the other side of the glass. Hood up, rain poured onto his body as he yelled, "Kate!" He pounded on the window hard enough that it would surely break.

"No!" Kate screamed as she sat up in bed, waking from her nightmare.

It was a nightmare.

IT WASN'T OFTEN Kate had nightmares anymore. But when she did, she ended up drenched in a pool of sweat, unable to fall back to sleep. It had been years since her assault, so she didn't hesitate to take melatonin to help her fall back to sleep and stay sleeping.

Kate's bedroom was on the second story of the house she owned. It was part of why she got a two-story house—so she wouldn't be on the ground level like in her nightmare, like what happened when she was a child.

Second grade was a rollercoaster for Kate. While it started great being in the same class as her best friend Amy, it was also the year when the boy who lived on the next block over started abusing her. The neighborhood kids played tag, touch-football, and ghost in the graveyard all evening, nearly every evening until the streetlights came on. When the streetlights came on, it was time to go home.

John Miller was older than Kate Sampson by four years. Though he wasn't a huge kid, he still towered over her. The streetlights came on one evening in early July, but John didn't want to stop playing. The other neighborhood kids went home, and John announced to their friends that he would walk Kate home. But instead of just walking her home, he told her he had something to show her in the trees along the way. That's when it happened for the first time. He pushed her into a tree, kissing her, leaving her stunned with no idea what was happening. When she tried to get away, he pinned her to the ground, tore down her shorts, and raped her inside the woods, not more than one hundred yards from her house.

Afterward, he waited until she composed herself then walked her the rest of the way home. "You know, I know where you live, Sampson. Obviously. You can't tell anyone about this. I'll kill your dog if you do," he'd threatened. "You don't want Max to die, do you? Don't make me prove it."

She stared at him, speechless, with tears in her eyes. Her

heart was pounding, and her body hurt. She didn't understand what had happened, but she knew she didn't want
him to kill Max.

When Kate got home, she went straight upstairs to her
bedroom because she knew she would break down and cry
if her parents confronted her. She didn't want to put Max at
risk.

Kate threw herself on her bed and sobbed into her
pillow so no one would hear. She heard scratches at her
door and eventually let Max in. She became too exhausted
to continue crying, so she lay there with Max, trying to
process. That's when she noticed the wetness in her underwear. She went to the bathroom and gasped in terror as she
saw blood in her underwear and dried streaks of it down
her legs. She cried again, not knowing what to do or if she
was going to die. Max was in the bathroom with her and laid
his head on her lap.

"It's okay, Max. I won't tell. I love you so much," Kate said
as she stroked his head, tears disappearing into his black
fur. She wrapped her underwear in toilet paper and stuck
them at the bottom of the wastebasket in the cabinet under
the sink. "No one has to know."

KATE WAS RAPED INTERMITTENTLY for a year. The final time it
happened, John had crawled through her bedroom window,
waking her in the middle of the night. It was storming
outside, much like in her nightmare, so he was drenched
from the rain. He knew her mom wouldn't hear him come
inside over the sound of the thunder.

John was out late because his parents didn't care where
he was. Before Kate could scream upon seeing him in her
bedroom, his hand was covering her mouth, and he whis-

pered, "How do you think Max wants to die? A bullet right between his eyes? A knife across his throat? Drowned in the creek?"

She shook her head violently, unable to speak. *No, no, no!* As a scared, only child, she didn't know what to do. But she loved Max, so she complied.

The abuse only stopped because John's mom moved him to Iowa with her when his parents split up. It was the most amazing news Kate had ever been told.

Thinking back on her childhood abuse, Kate recognized the reaction she had in her state of panic. Not fight, flight, or freeze. It was *appease.* She had complied. She did what she was told. As a naive child, she couldn't rationalize any other choice. Max was everything to her, so she needed to protect him. And she did by giving up the protection she should have had for herself.

8

TUESDAY, JUNE 22, 2021

6:15 p.m.

Brian had gone back to his house with lavender walls after leaving Julie's. He opened the garage door, parked his car, and went inside carrying an empty beer bottle.

A bottle of Jack Daniel's waited for him on the counter. He smiled at the instant chill he felt with his air conditioner set at sixty-seven degrees Fahrenheit. He took off his suit jacket, tossed it over a cheap folding chair next to the card table he used as a kitchen table, then pulled out a glass from the cupboard—ice, then Jack Daniel's, then Coke.

He made his way to the living room, which housed only a single chair and a TV on a cheap wooden stand. He propped his feet onto the cardboard box he used as a foot-stool and switched on the TV.

9

8:22 p.m.

A large box was waiting on Kate's doorstep when she got home after closing the store. She neared the door and noticed it was her SimpliSafe Security System.

"Hey! Guess what I got in the mail today," Kate said into the phone, Amy listening from the other end.

"Uh, a letter from a long-lost half-sister you never knew you had?"

"No! My security system. Zan volunteered you guys to help me put it up."

"For sure. She won't be home from work until ten o'clock tonight. You okay to wait till tomorrow?" Amy asked.

"Sure thing. I've gone this long without one. What's another day going to hurt?" Kate said.

The next afternoon, Kate, Amy, and Zan were sitting on the back patio having a light beer with green olives, enjoying the seventy-five-degree weather after successfully installing Kate's new security system.

They put window sensors on all of her windows, strategically placed panic buttons, a couple of cameras, a motion detector, and a glass-break sensor. They mounted the keypad on the wall next to her front door to unlock the system upon entering her home.

"This is the first murder we've had like this since I've been with the Winona County Police Department. I mean, almost every other murder that's happened around here has been gang or drug-related. We've found no evidence that these women were into drugs or owed anyone money. Their records were clean. And we're still trying to figure out if it was the same guy who raped both women. Whoever he is, he's been pretty damn good at covering his tracks and staying hidden," Zan said.

"Good thing Winona has the best of the best on their team," Kate said.

"Awe, thanks, Sampson," Zan replied, slapping Kate on the knee.

"I meant Douglas!" Kate joked.

Amy and Kate burst out laughing at Zan's expense.

"I'm so glad you can take a joke, babe," Amy told Zan.

"So, you guys might think I'm crazy, but I went on a bit of a shopping spree the other day after watching the press release about that girl, Stacie," Kate added.

"Did you max out your credit card at the liquor store again?" Zan joked, trying to take a stab back at Kate.

"Oh yeah. Fourth time this year!" Kate laughed. "Nah, I got a few of those cat ear keychains. You know, the ones you put on your pointer and middle finger, kind of like brass knuckles, except they are pointed like cat ears. And a knife. And pepper spray. Two pepper sprays, rather."

Amy and Zan raised their eyebrows at Kate but sighed in agreement. Zan said, "Yeah, you can never be too careful." She had always been an advocate for personal safety. "You still got that softball bat from summer league last year?"

"Yeah," Kate said.

"Put it in the entryway of your house. Tuck it right inside that closet or something," Zan suggested. Kate nodded that she would.

Amy and Zan left to have dinner with Amy's folks, and Kate stayed productive around her house, listening to her favorite podcast. The sun beat down on her back as she stood on a step stool, reaching up for the light bulb that had burned out on her front porch string of lights. Barely reaching, Kate grabbed the bulb, but upon grasping it, the stool tipped, kicking out from under her. She landed hard on the ground with a thunderous thud.

Someone ran over from the house next door. "I'm okay! I'm okay," Kate declared, moaning and groaning into a sitting position, noticing someone was on their way. She looked up and recognized who had run over to her house. It was the man from the store the other day, the one who bought her favorite book. He was wearing a cut-off tank top, revealing the lion tattoo on his left shoulder, the cat she thought she saw under his sleeve the other day.

"Hey. You sure you're okay?" he asked as he jogged to her front porch, immediately recognizing her too. He reached out a hand to help her up.

Grasping his hand, she replied, "Thanks. Yeah, I'm fine. I mean, my pride has been destroyed, but I don't think anything is broken." She smiled, embarrassed. "That damn bulb burned out, and I don't have a ladder. I should. I sell them at my store, yet I still don't have one," Kate said disheveled, pointing at the bulb she was trying to get to.

"I tell you what. I have a ladder. Let me go grab it, ok?" he replied.

"Sure," she said, appreciative of his benevolence and surprised at herself for accepting the help from a stranger. She noticed the definition in his shoulders and arms as he walked back toward his house.

Wait. The house. His house. He's the new neighbor? She questioned to herself.

A moment later, he returned with his ladder, standing it under her broken bulb. He climbed up with ease, and Kate couldn't help but notice his neon orange tennis shoes. *Who wears orange shoes?* She said nothing but giggled to herself. He unscrewed the bulb, handing it down to her. She looked up at him with a gentle smile and handed him the replacement.

"Thank you, seriously. I don't usually ask for help. But it looks like I need to get myself a ladder," Kate said, ashamed.

"Nah, don't worry about it. Besides, you didn't ask for help. I offered. That's what neighbors are for," he replied, descending the ladder. She was surprised at how much he talked now compared to when they met in the store.

"Kate," she offered, extending a hand.

"Kevin," he said, taking her hand, smiling upon touching it. "Alright, well, let me know if you need anything else, okay?"

"Will do," she said as he turned to walk away. "Hey, wait a second. Question for you. Why did you take down your porch lights?"

"Remember how I said I'm surprised the house hadn't burned down yet? I was going to fix them up with electrical tape, but they're so bad, I'm going to replace them instead. I'll have them back up by the weekend, I'm sure," he said.

"You must be into lights?" He scanned hers that ran across her entire porch.

"Oh, you noticed? Yeah, I am," Kate said, smiling. "The old neighbors were pretty cheap people, so that doesn't really surprise me. They fixed everything they could themselves before replacing anything. Let me know if you need help," Kate said.

"Sure thing. Have a good day, Kate," Kevin replied. He had a charming, country-boy accent and smile, but she kept her wall up and kept her distance, waiting for the kindness to fade as it did with most men she'd met.

His tank top blew gently in the breeze as he walked away, revealing a small portion of his chest where she saw another tattoo. *An owl, maybe?*

"See ya later, Kevin."

That night, while lying in bed, Kate's phone made an alert noise. She reached over to it, picked it up, and read, "Motion detected. Front door camera."

Huh?

Goosebumps flooded her arms, and a chill consumed her entire body. Her heart raced, pumping adrenaline through her veins. The blade from her nightstand was in her hand in a matter of seconds before she opened the alarm system app on her phone. The camera that doubled as a doorbell showed one recent recording. She continued to grip the knife as she waited for the video to load. Once it did, she watched a forty-five-second video of a figure moving across her porch, right in front of the door.

What the hell was that?

10

FRIDAY, JUNE 25, 2021

9:00 a.m.

"Why did you come to work when you have a fever, Ashley?" Kate asked with her eyebrows clenched, confused. Ashley hadn't been vaccinated yet, but she had her appointment set for the first dose the following week.

"I don't know. I mean, I didn't know I had a fever until I just checked it. I felt chills earlier, but I thought it was just because it was cold this morning. I made an appointment to get tested for COVID-19. I'll let you know as soon as I have the results," Ashley explained before leaving. "And yes, I still have my appointment to get vaccinated next week! There's no way in hell I'm canceling that appointment." Alex had pulled up to the front of the store to pick her up but stayed waiting in his car.

Kate and Ashley hadn't been sick yet, but Nancy got COVID-19 over Christmas of 2020. She never found out who she got it from, but that ultimately didn't matter. She fought for her life in the ICU and barely made it out alive. The doctors considered intubating her, but she miraculously started perking up before they went through with it. Nancy was one of those women who seemed to face the worst yet survived everything, and she did it again with COVID-19.

Despite the high percentage of vaccinations in the area, there were still few cases of COVID-19 hitting people who hadn't been vaccinated. Kate disinfected every surface she thought Ashley might have touched and went into work mode.

EARLIER THAT MORNING, Kate woke up with the sun. It beamed in through her window, through the one small crack between her blackout curtains. Her wicker chair was on the porch, and a new canvas was calling her name, willing her to get out of bed. She thought of pink, purple, blue, and green paints as she dreamed of the place she wanted to be—in Alaska watching the sunset turn into the evening's Northern Lights. It was something she'd always dreamed of seeing. Despite the cold morning she woke up to, it was going to be a beautiful day. Checking the weather made her wonder what it would feel like in Alaska this time of year. She tried to think of the temperatures as she planned the colors of her painting.

There was no podcast, music, or company that morning, just simply the fresh morning air and the scene she was creating. She sat on her front sidewalk near the flower bed, brushing the canvas with green and a touch of blue. Two hours flew by, and she'd run out of forest green, a color that her canvas would be incomplete without.

When Kate went to the store to grab paint, she didn't realize she'd have to stay for the rest of the day to replace Ashley. The cream canvas, her favorite thing to paint on, was at home waiting for her. Hawaiian sunsets, tropical islands,

Montana mountains, and the ocean she remembers her mother taking her to when she was young were all painted on a canvas hung somewhere in the store or in her home. While Kate painted places she'd been, she always loved painting scenes of places she wished she had been—far away from reality, far away from the memories that haunted her.

It was fine being at work until six o'clock that evening when the clouds rolled in, showering sprinkles of rain on the windows of her store. *Rain was not in the forecast,* she thought. All of her supplies and canvas stayed on the sidewalk while she was gone. And now she was stuck, unable to go home to put them inside. *It's fine, s*he thought. That seemed to become her motto. Not only was there rain, the small but intense storm also brought thunder and lightning. Julie's was far more important than her canvas, so she went about her business, greeting her customers as though nothing else was on her mind.

THE STORE never closed a minute before 8:00 p.m. with exception of the holidays. It had always been her mom's rule, and Kate kept the tradition going. But as soon as eight o'clock hit, the sign went off, the lights went out, and Kate locked the door behind her.

It had stopped raining, and she was able to walk home dry. Cat ears were ready to go in her hand on the walk to her porch where the lights were on, waiting for her. Kate was about to enter the code on her new smart lock when she suddenly stopped.

Wait. Where is my canvas? She asked herself.

She looked right—nothing. She looked left, and there it was. Her wicker chair, paints, and canvas stood with a sheet draped over the top of her almost-complete painting of Northern Lights. *Maybe Zan or Amy stopped by*.

She removed the sheet and grabbed the canvas off its stand to take it inside when she saw a small piece of torn paper under her paintbrush cup.

I didn't think you meant to leave this in the rain. - Kevin

Kevin. Even though he'd taken down his porch lights, Kate thought maybe having him as a neighbor wouldn't be so bad after all.

11

FALL 1995

It was a war zone. Epic battles were starring Natalie and Chuck, often because of substance abuse and the aftermath. Natalie had been too hungover to go to work one evening, and Chuck was banking on using the tips she was going to make to pay for cocaine he'd gotten the week prior. When he got home and realized she hadn't left, he punched a hole through the hallway closet door after a vicious screaming match. It was a hole that would stay in that door for months to come, reminding Nate of how afraid he felt that night hiding under his covers.

Natalie had never used drugs before Nate's father dying. It was Joe's death that struck her curiosity about substances. She had tried to cope on her own with an infant son but quickly learned alcohol worked better to drown her sorrows and wash away the moments she shared with Joe, who she so dearly missed. Binge drinking got her in with the wrong crowd, who then introduced her to drugs. Meeting Chuck enabled her to continue using. Not only did he not stop her destructive behavior, but he also encouraged her to continue using simply because it was the way he lived too.

The fighting, accompanied by his fear, consumed Nate's life. No longer was he just the neglected child, but also the abused child. Nothing was ever good enough, and his mom had nearly given up sticking up for him all together. What she didn't know was the abuse Nate endured behind his closed bedroom door.

It had become a regular thing. At least once a week, Nate was sexually abused by Chuck. Each week that passed, Nate became more cold, numb, and broken. He could not fight the man that weighed four times as much as him, the man that threatened to hurt his mother if he told. Although Natalie kept Nate in this living situation, he knew he still had to protect her. But he grew more resentful toward her each day that passed.

IN JANUARY OF 1996, Chuck had thrown Nate so hard against the counter that he went unconscious as soon as his head hit the edge. Natalie, not sober enough to drive, called paramedics. An ambulance came and immediately put a cervical collar on Nate, stabilizing his unconscious body and strapping him to a stretcher. Chuck eyed Natalie as she went with the EMT to the ambulance. It was a look that said, *Watch yourself.* The ambulance took Nate and his mother to the local ER. Deputies stayed at the house interrogating Chuck, who told the story of how Nate was playing around on top of the counter and fell off, hitting his head on the floor.

Nate was kept in a medically induced coma until the swelling on his brain went down. A deputy had come by the hospital to talk with Natalie. She told him she was not in the room when Nate was injured, so she wasn't sure what had happened. It was all she could come up with. She went over in her mind what would happen if she had told the truth. Would Chuck kill her? Would he kill Nate? Would they be living in the street since he took over her home?

Days later, he woke up surrounded by monitors, an Intensive Care Unit nurse, and his mother. But upon waking up, it was evident that the light in his eyes had turned to a dusky gray. He no longer had the spirit of a small child that he once carried. He became dark, quiet, and cold.

Nearly a week went by where Nate was in the ICU under close observation before he was released to go home. He was fed well, checked on, and treated with kindness by the nurses. His mom stayed with him nearly the whole time. Social services were involved in determining if Nate experienced abused or if Chuck's story was true. Natalie left the room, leaving a social worker alone with Nate.

"Nate, my name is Hilary. I want to talk to you about what happened before you came into the hospital. Is that okay?" She was a well-put-together Asian-American woman in black slacks and a black blazer. Her demeanor was warm and motherly, easily comforting Nate.

Nate didn't respond with words, only a small nod of his head.

"Do you remember what happened before your mom called the ambulance?" she asked.

Again, he had no words. All Nate did was gently shake his head no.

"I understand. It sounds like you had a concussion. That's quite traumatic. Have you ever had a concussion before?"

Nate shrugged his shoulders, looking up at her.

After some more small talk, she asked, "Do you feel safe at home, Nate?"

The question struck Nate. Was it an opportunity for him to be honest? Was it a test? Would Chuck find out what he says? So many options went through his mind, but for fear of what might happen if the truth got out, Nate shook his head yes. But it was so subtle; she had to ask.

"You feel safe at home?" she verified.

Again, he nodded his head, yes.

After a dozen more questions, the social worker had nothing else to go by other than the story Chuck was telling and the vague answers from Nate.

He knew the story that Chuck had told authorities, and he knew it wasn't true. But he went with it because that seemed like the easiest thing to do. He didn't want to be taken away from his mom or get her in trouble, so he pretended things were fine at home. The threats Chuck instilled into Nate's head overpowered the thought of telling the truth. The only physical injury the nurses and doctors could see was on his head. Unfortunately, being sexually abused as a child gave him injuries they couldn't see upon a simple physical examination.

The other part of being hospitalized Nate enjoyed was seeing his mother sober. She'd been trying to quit substance abuse and find the courage to leave Chuck. This time, the withdrawal symptoms weren't as bad as the last few times she'd tried to quit. Natalie staying by Nate's side in the hospital made him almost believe she would leave Chuck.

But upon returning home, Nate quickly learned that she would not.

Chuck's aggression toward Natalie had become more noteworthy. Earlier that summer, Nate watched Chuck hold his mom against the wall with one hand around her throat, pinning her there as he yelled, watching her struggle to breathe.

Another time, he used the vacuum cord as a tool for strangulation when Natalie took the cash stored in the jar on top of the fridge. He accused her of buying drugs and hiding them. She denied this but still wouldn't tell Chuck the truth, that she would use the money to get Nate a bike for his birthday. Instead of using Nate as the reason for her sneaking around, she kept her reasonings to herself.

Chuck had wrapped the cord around her neck from behind. "How does it feel, Natalie? Huh? Do you like this? Does it feel good, like the drugs you hid from me? How did they feel?" he demanded. "Was it worth this? Huh?"

Natalie flailed her arms, grabbing at his forearms while shaking her head no.

"You're a worthless, pathetic excuse for a human. You have a shit job and no money. All you have is that worthless son of yours who can't handle a little punishment and criticism, and now you have hospital bills to pay because of it. You're pathetic," he finished and threw her on the ground, releasing the vacuum cord. He spat on her as she laid there, then made himself a drink at the kitchen counter.

"Pathetic," he said, still mumbling remarks when Natalie had regained enough strength to crawl to her phone and head toward Nate's room to call the authorities.

As dispatch answered, "Nine-one-one, what's your emergency?" Natalie closed Nate's door quietly behind her, locking the knob.

"Please come. My boyfriend almost killed me," she whispered, her voice trembling. "Please, hurry."

Natalie looked over her shoulder and saw her son sitting on his bed cross-legged, simply staring at her. "Oh, honey," she cried. He'd been sitting in his room listening to their entire fight, but he was emotionless as he watched her cry into the phone.

"I'm so sorry, honey. I'm so, so sorry," she said, hugging him tightly. *What have I done?*

Chuck was arrested that day and taken to County Jail. When he was allowed phone privileges, he called Natalie. "Babe. You know I was coming down," he said, referring to coming down from his high. "I didn't mean any of that. You know me, babe," he said, sweet-talking her and begging her to take him back.

"I'd do anything for you. We've been trying to clean up for so long. Let's do it this time. Let's do it together. I'll change for you," he promised. "It's okay that you took the money. We'll make it back," he said.

"Chuck, I didn't use that money for drugs. I was going to buy Nate a bike for his birthday," she finally explained.

"Oh, good!" he said in a high-pitched voice. Natalie wondered if he was being fake, but then he continued, "Buy him the bike. In fact, if it wasn't enough money, we'll make more, and you can buy him a really nice one. We'll be just fine, babe. I promise."

Somehow this got to her, and she saw a glimpse of good in him. She still loved him even though she hated him. But it wasn't *him* she loved. It was who she thought he could be. It was the small glimpse of a good human he rarely portrayed that she held on to, wishing every day his goodness would come around more often. She loved the rare moments when he was kind, caring, and looked at her as though she were the most beautiful girl in the world.

She dropped the domestic assault charges, and Nate got his new bike. When Chuck returned home, things quickly went back to normal. Except this time, he threatened to kill her and Nate if she ever called the police again. He was adamant they could work out their differences amongst themselves without the cops.

ONE LAST TIME, Nate begged his mom to leave Chuck.

"Honey, things will turn around. We're going to be better. You'll see," she promised him. All he could do was look up at her with his cold eyes, knowing what she said wasn't the truth. She still did not know Chuck was hurting Nate when she left for work or after she'd gone to bed at night.

The warmth Nate once had in his soul was gone completely now, taken over by rage. It was a feeling he didn't understand or know how to express.

Summer 1996

Nate had turned eleven in the summer of 1996. He continued to stay out of sight as much as possible, doing his chores, and looking forward to nothing other than returning to school in the fall, where he would get breakfast, lunch, and an afternoon snack. The dusky gray eyes Nate woke up from his coma with had turned stone cold. The light in his soul had faded, revealing darkness and resentment he'd house for the rest of his life.

On the morning of the first school day, Nate acted as though it was just another day. He got himself cereal, put on his mismatched socks and tennis shoes that were falling apart, and stood in the doorway debating about waking up his mom to say goodbye.

He didn't. Instead, Nate opened the trailer door and headed down the wooden steps before making his way up the gravel road. It would have been a left turn to wait at the bus stop with the other kids, but that day, he went right.

The entire weekend he had been anxiously anticipating that morning. He'd only have a couple of hours to get as far away from there as possible before the school called his mom, wondering where he was. He filled his backpack with clothes and his precious belongings, including his yellow blankie and the half-completed baby book his mom had started before she found a love for drugs. Underneath his bed housed the schoolbooks that should have been in his backpack for the first day of school.

He never saw those books again.

12

SATURDAY, JUNE 26, 2021

8:07 a.m.

The investigation of the murder of Stacie was still underway. Investigators had sent samples to the state for DNA testing, as well as fingerprints from the doorknob, in hopes they'd be able to link the samples with someone already in the system. Deputies worked around the clock, collecting evidence and analyzing it, using all methods and resources necessary.

A woman named Amber, who was around the same age as Stacie, had been violently raped by an unknown, masked man in her home in the middle of the night weeks before Stacie's murder. Since incidents like this were so rare in southeastern Minnesota, there was suspicion it was the same criminal in both cases. They needed to determine the link between the two women and if this was the work of the same monster so they could put him behind bars before he hurt anyone else.

Zan was driving to the crime scene when she passed Kate's house. She pulled into the driveway after seeing Kate sitting on her porch painting. "Kate. Isn't it too early for this?" Zan asked, teasing as she stepped out of her car and made her way up to Kate's sidewalk.

"It's never too early to start your day with happiness, Deputy Ramiro!" Kate replied, too cheerful for it being so early in the morning. She was sitting in a light blue summer dress, nothing on her feet and no makeup on.

"What do you have going on today?" Zan asked.

Kate replied, "Who wants to know?" eyeing her curiously, then laughing. "I'm taking the day off. Nancy is at the store. Ashley's COVID-19 results came back negative, and she's already feeling better. She plans to work tonight so here I am, seizing the day."

"Okay, good. We'll pick you up at six," Zan told her.

Kate raised an eyebrow and asked, "You and Amy? Where are we going?"

"Newts in Rochester. You need a good burger and a pile of fries on those bones," Zan replied.

"Fine! That actually sounds really good," Kate said, perking up. "Hey, I met the neighbor last night."

"Oh, yeah? Are they old and grumpy? Homophobes? What's the scoop?" Zan questioned.

"His name is Kevin. He saved my ass when I was trying to change one of these damn light bulbs," she said, pointing to the porch lights. "He's kind of sexy too, like the rugged type. You know what I mean? He doesn't seem to care to impress anyone."

"Uh, yeah. Yep. Sure do," Zan said, rolling her eyes. "So when do I get to meet this Kevin guy?"

"Oh, knock it off. Never. You never get to. Go away. Don't you have a bad guy to find?" Kate teased.

"Yeah, that's why I came by. How's your security system working? All good?"

"Seems to work fine. It did record a motion detected from the doorbell last night, though. Something ran across my porch. I obviously didn't sleep after that, but I didn't see anything when I looked outside from my bedroom upstairs. I assumed it was someone's dog that got out or something. It was weird and so close to the doorbell I just couldn't tell what it was," Kate said, pulling out her phone to show Zan the video. They leaned their heads in together to watch.

"What the hell is that? I'll have the crew keep an eye on your house. We don't have any leads on Stacie's murderer. But whoever he is, he's just roaming around out there like a lion in a field of deer." Zan paused. Kate looked at Zan wide-eyed as the color in her face drained.

"Sorry, I probably shouldn't have said that," Zan said. "Let me know if you need anything, though. Alright?"

"You got it, boss," Kate murmured. She managed to salute Zan sarcastically as she turned around and headed back toward her squad car.

"Six o'clock, woman!" Zan said as she got in her car.

AT 6:04 P.M., Kate was waiting by the window for Zan and Amy. *Always late,* she thought. *Typical.* She'd curled her hair, put on a dash of blush, two coats of mascara, neutral eyeshadow, and a tinted Chapstick. It wasn't all too often Kate went out. Not that she didn't want to. She was just busy with the store, her house, and sometimes she simply preferred to paint.

Paint-by-numbers started her obsession. After she was assaulted as a child, she inadvertently found activities to help keep her mind occupied. They were things that helped her cope. Being too young to rationalize what coping was, she simply realized painting required just enough attention to keep her focus on what she was actively doing to forget the trauma she endured. She had been given a paint-by-numbers canvas with fresh paint and brushes for Christmas when she was in second grade. Within only a few days, she'd completed the entire canvas.

After Julie found out about the abuse, she got Kate more canvases. Anything that helped her heal, she would make work regardless of how much it cost. Julie only found out Kate had been abused because Kate had broken down to Amy after John and his mom left. Not knowing what to do, Amy told her mom, who then told Kate's mom. Kate was angry at first because she thought John would come back to kill Max, but Julie worked through this with Kate, telling her it wasn't true, and she wouldn't let that happen.

The heartache of knowing her daughter had been abused for so long hurt Julie more than anything she'd ever experienced. She cried hysterically behind a closed bathroom door after Amy's mom hung up the phone. She'd gotten Kate into therapy right away and did everything she could to facilitate her healing. The store wasn't doing so well, but Kate was her number one priority.

ZAN AND AMY pulled up to Kate's house just past 6:15 p.m., honking twice as if Kate wasn't standing at the window already waiting for them. She set her alarm and locked her door behind her. Newts was a local restaurant in Rochester owned by local people, but it was so successful, they opened two additional locations.

"Light beer with olives, please," Amy told the waitress.

"Make that two," Zan added.

"Three," said Kate.

An hour later, their burgers were gone, and they were on their second round of beers.

"So she was in the shower and all of a sudden, I heard this blood-curdling scream. I thought she was dying!" Zan said about Amy.

"Knock it off. It wasn't that bad!" Amy defended herself.

"It was a spider on the shower wall!" Zan went on. "Next thing I know, Amy's running out of the bathroom butt-ass naked while I'm talking to my parents in the kitchen!"

"How the hell was I supposed to know they were stopping by?" Amy questioned.

"She was running right toward us, and when she realized I was talking to my parents, she turned and ran into the hallway closet!" Zan finished, laughing so hard Kate could hardly understand her. "It was so funny!"

Kate was laughing too, so much that she had tears in the corner of her eyes. She always loved the idea of being a fly on the wall in their home.

"Oh my gosh. You guys crack me up. I gotta go break the seal," Kate said as she stood and headed toward the bathroom. A few minutes later, she rounded the corner and ran into someone on her way out.

"Oh, excuse me!" she said, looking up to see who she'd nearly tackled coming out of the bathroom.

"Hello, Kate." It was Brian, the man she met at the store. He smiled before continuing, "That was my fault. How are you?" he asked, still holding onto his confident demeanor.

"Good, just having dinner with a couple of girlfriends," Kate replied.

Brian hesitated for only a moment before taking a breath and asking, "I was thinking about you after I left your store the other day. I was kicking myself for not asking for your phone number. And now, here we are."

"Yes, here we are," Kate replied hesitantly but smiling.

Brian went on, "So, I don't see a ring on your finger. May I ask you to have lunch with me tomorrow?"

Kate had gone on dates here and there, but she hadn't had a boyfriend in years. She used the store as an excuse to get out of going to social events more often than not. She believed heartbreak couldn't happen if she didn't let anyone get too close, but his confidence and charisma invited her to let her guard down just enough to accept the offer.

"Sure, why not? Do you have somewhere in mind?"

"Don't sound so excited," he teased. "I do. How about I pick you up at noon?"

Kate contemplated for just a moment if she should instead ask to meet him somewhere. But she didn't. He was well put together and she somehow trusted this stranger enough to let him pick her up. "That works for me. I'll text you my address." She handed him her phone, "Type in your number."

Once he was done, she took her phone back and noticed him smile at her before saying, "Okay, great. I'll see you tomorrow, Kate."

"See you tomorrow," she replied.

Kate was glowing. When she went back to the table, the girls asked, "Jesus, did you fall in? What happened in there?" They paused for only a moment before noticing her glow. "Wait, why are you smiling?"

"I ran into a guy I met at the store the other day. He's new to town and so handsome. His name is Brian," Kate said with a sigh and a smirk on her slightly flushed face.

"Not your neighbor, though, right? What's his name again? Corey?" Zan questioned.

"No, no. My neighbor is Kevin," Kate replied.

"That's right! You know, Amy mentioned she knows a Kevin and wondered if it was the same guy as your neighbor," Zan said, looking toward her wife.

"Does he have a couple of tattoos? A lion and an owl?" Amy asked.

"Kevin? He does, actually. You know him?" Kate replied.

"Kevin Winter! I do know him!" Amy said excitedly. "Oh boy, we go way back. I used to play with him and his brother when we were little. I haven't seen him in ages, but we're friends on social media. I'll have to come by and see him sometime. I miss him. He was always so nice and sweet."

"That's good news, considering he lives right next door to me," Kate said with relief. "Too bad he wasn't around when you guys were over the other day. Anyway, I'm having lunch with Brian tomorrow."

Zan and Amy eyed each other, clearly surprised. "Well, good for you!" Amy exclaimed in her always optimistic tone. "Are you excited?"

"Yes, but no. I really don't *need* to add anyone to my life," Kate started.

Before she could go any further, Zan interrupted. "We know you don't *need* anyone, Kate. You're the most badass bitch I've ever met. But that doesn't mean you can't have some fun. Be straight up. Tell him you just want to be casual."

"I'll give it a whirl," Kate replied.

"What are you guys doing for your first date?" Amy asked, overly curious.

"He's going to pick me up at noon. I guess he has somewhere he wants to take me for lunch." Amy and Zan looked at each other again, somehow knowing they were both thinking the same thing.

"So you gave Brian your address, I take it?" Zan asked.

Kate paused and blushed, appearing as if she didn't know what to say. "I did. I don't know what I was thinking. I almost told him I'd just meet him somewhere, but I didn't want to be rude," she said.

"That wouldn't have been rude, Sampson. Just be careful, ok?" Zan said, eyeing Kate.

"You guys. This is why I don't date. I have no idea what I'm doing," Kate said, disappointed with herself.

"Don't worry, we'll keep an eye on you," Amy added. She turned and smiled at Zan, who was trying to hide her obvious concern.

13

SUNDAY, JUNE 27, 2021

12:00 p.m.

His silver car pulled into Kate's driveway at exactly noon. *Hm, a man who knows how to be on time,* she thought. She jotted down his license plate number and left it on the table by her front door. Brian got out of his car and walked up to Kate's door, ringing the doorbell. She waited a moment, then opened the door, revealing the pink and white dress that hugged her body in all of the right places, with her hair loosely curled, falling over her shoulders.

She watched his eyes find hers. He smiled before saying, "Wow, you look great."

Kate immediately blushed, enjoying the compliment. "Thanks. You do too." He was wearing dark jeans and a dress shirt. Not too casual, but not too fancy. They walked to his car, where he opened his passenger door for her.

"Thank you." She smiled at him.

They went to Rochester, where they had a delicious lunch at a nice place on the west side of town. They sat on the patio in the shade and had a simple conversation. Kate had a glass of Sangria, and Brian had two tall beers. Her face was flushed after one drink as he ordered a third.

"I was married before," Brian said out of nowhere. "She always took forever to get ready to leave the house and had to have a purse that matched her outfit." Kate stared at him, not knowing what to say.

"Were you ever married?" he asked Kate.

"No. Truthfully, I haven't dated in a while," she replied.

"How come?" he asked.

She sighed and thought about what to say before replying. "I have a hard time trusting people. And when I do, it just doesn't seem to work out. I end up regretting that I trusted them."

A moment later, she was being hugged from behind by Ashley.

"Hey, beautiful!" Ashley said to Kate.

"If your COVID hadn't come back as negative yet, I'd be so mad at you right now." Kate teased. Ashley and Alex were being seated at a table right next to Kate and Brian.

"Alex, Ashley, this is Brian," Kate introduced him.

"Nice to meet you both," Brian said, shaking their hands. He didn't seem thrilled as he quickly sat down after introducing himself.

"Nice to meet you too," Alex said. Alex wasn't very tall, just a couple of inches taller than Kate, and his blond, shaggy hair made him look like a surfer. "What's good?"

"The Buffalo Wontons are to die for!" Kate said, glancing at Brian to figure out what his face was trying to say. It was unusual how his confident demeanor had suddenly changed to being so uncomfortable.

The server stopped by with Brian's beer and took Ashley and Alex's order.

"I'll have a Whiskey Sour, and she'll have the same," he

said, ordering for Ashley. Kate raised an eyebrow at this, not realizing the dominance he held over Ashley. He usually looked thrown together and rough around the edges, but today he looked more like a prom date with his new black slacks that looked two sizes too big and a button-down shirt that also looked a bit oversized. Ashley gave a small smile, nodding her head that whiskey would be fine.

Kate was glad to have more people around her. She was feeling a bit uncomfortable being flushed after just one drink. Brian finished his third beer before getting up to go to the bathroom again.

As Ashley and Alex got their lunch, Brian and Kate were paying the bill to leave. "It was good to see you two," Kate said, smiling at them both.

"Good to see you," Alex replied.

Ashley stood and hugged Kate, "Have a good night. Let me know if you need anything, okay?"

"Always. Bye!" Kate replied. Brian glared at Ashley and Alex for a split second before turning and walking toward the door with Kate leading.

His car stayed mostly between the lines as heavy rock played through the speakers, a sound Kate wasn't used to. They arrived back at Kate's house, and both got out of the car. He walked over to her and swayed just slightly as he said, "Thank you for coming to lunch with me, Kate. Maybe we can see each other again sometime?"

"I'd be okay with that," Kate hesitantly smiled, concerned that he shouldn't be driving after three tall beers in such a short amount of time. Kate didn't know what else to say, so she turned to walk toward her house. Suddenly, Brian grabbed her hand and pulled her toward him, bringing her in for a kiss. He put his arm around her waist as his lips met hers. She was surprised, but she didn't push him away. After a moment, he pulled his lips away from hers and said, "See you later."

He smiled at her, then got into his car and drove away. Kate was left standing there, speechless, trying to process what had just happened.

14

SUNDAY, JUNE 27, 2021

3:00 p.m.

Brian arrived home, pulling into the garage and closing the door behind him. He stepped out of his car, stumbled just slightly as he headed into his house, into the frigid air and darkness.

He pulled a glass out of his cupboard and set it on the counter—ice, then Jack Daniels, then Coke. Instead of putting his feet up, he went to the kitchen table, where he opened his laptop to work. He took a sip of his drink as he pulled up Internet Explorer, where he'd saved the last article he was looking at, "Woman Raped, Murdered, Found in her Bathtub."

15

5:30 p.m.

It was the seventh-inning stretch of the Twins game. Amy loved the surprise tickets and the Ellen DeGeneres book. Zan was winning.

"You're the best," Amy said, kissing Zan on the cheek.

But Amy was winning too. She had her mom make a quilt out of Amy and Zan's t-shirts from when they were kids, and she gave it to Zan as an anniversary gift. Zan, who was tough as nails, was fighting tears when she opened it.

Zan's smartwatch vibrated. Deputy McGriff's name came up as the incoming call. She ignored it, wanting to spend the evening with her beautiful wife for their second wedding anniversary. The vibrating stopped. Zan took a drink of her beer as Amy jumped up from her chair when the Twins scored another run.

McGriff's name popped up on Zan's watch again.

"Hey, babe," Zan said to Amy. "McGriff has called twice now. I'm going to answer this, okay?"

"Of course." Amy always supported Zan's career.

Zan answered, "You know, I'm at the Twins game with my wife for our anniversary. What could be so important, McGriff?"

"Calm down. You'll want to hear this. I was looking through evidence from the first rape case. Nothing stuck out to me until I noticed a small bag with a white rose petal in it. They had questioned the victim, Amber, about it, and she said she hadn't had any white roses in her house around that time, if ever." He dramatically paused. "Zan. It's the same type of petal found at our murder scene."

"Holy shit," was all she could say.

WHEN THE TWINS won against the New York Yankees seven to four, Zan and Amy walked to their car to head back to Dover. Zan debated about saying anything since the case was still unsolved, but she felt like she would burst if she kept the information to herself. "Remember how I went to talk to McGriff?"

"Oh, yeah. What's he up to?" Amy asked nonchalantly.

"It's the same guy. The guy who raped the first victim, Amber, is the same guy who raped and murdered Stacie," Zan said, calm and cool, completely opposite of how she felt.

Amy turned to look at Zan, who was driving. She stared at her for a moment before asking, "What? Really? How do you know?"

"There was evidence found at both of the crime scenes. It was the same evidence in both places," Zan replied.

"Wow. Maybe you'll have more evidence between the two cases then," Amy said, blissfully hopeful. "What's the evidence?" she questioned.

Zan replied, "A white rose petal."

. . .

In Dover, Kate sat on her front porch swing reading a book written by the two female comedians from the podcast she loves. An hour passed, and she couldn't put the book down. The sunlight was fading as she heard her neighbor's front door open, and the screen slapped shut behind him.

Kevin stepped onto his front porch with a box in his arms. He'd gone to the garage and came back with a ladder he leaned against his house. He pulled new lights from the box and walked up the ladder without noticing Kate was next door peeking at him from the corner of her eye. He had brought a speaker out with him and turned on Chris Stapleton's song, *Tennessee Whiskey*. One of her favorites. As Kevin unboxed the string of lights on his porch, they stuck together in a tangle. It looked like a hard job to do solo, so Kate closed her book and walked over.

"Need a hand, neighbor?" she asked with a grin.

"I never ask for help," he mocked her.

Kate laughed out loud and grabbed the lights anyway, helping him untangle them. "New lights, huh? I like them. Very classy."

"Thanks, the neighbor next door has a thing against darkness, I guess, so I thought I better follow suit." He winked at her as the soothing music added to the charming tone of his voice.

They successfully hung up the new lights and plugged them in, but they didn't light up. "Well, what the hell? Maybe we should have made sure they worked before hanging them up."

"Check the breaker. I remember the last owners having to do that a lot," Kate said.

"No surprise," he said, walking to his garage. She

followed and smiled like a smartass as the lights came on when he flipped the breaker.

"Huh. Well good, because if these didn't work, I wasn't going to go buy more of them." He opened his garage fridge and grabbed a beer holding it toward her, "Beer? I feel like I owe you."

"Oh sure, you talked me into it," Kate said.

They went back to his front porch and sat on the steps. "So, what do you do for work?" Kate asked, taking a drink.

"I'm a superintendent for a construction company," Kevin replied.

"Ah, interesting. How do you like that?" Kate asked.

"I love it. I can still get my hands dirty, and I like staying busy. I've been running a handful of jobs for the past few months. I like keeping everything organized. Or, trying anyway," Kevin replied. "And you own a store?"

"Yeah, it was my mom's. She passed away," she replied.

"I'm so sorry to hear that."

"Thanks. It's been hard, but I've been keeping myself swamped with work, so I don't have to think about it. Which seems counterintuitive since I'm literally surrounded by my mom and her legacy every single day at work," she said, almost confusing herself. "Actually, I hear you know my friend Amy. You guys used to play together as kids?" Kate asked.

"Amy? Yeah! Wow, I haven't seen her in years."

"She said I better watch out for you," Kate teased.

"She knows me so well," Kevin said, going along with it.

Kate felt comfortable knowing they had been friends. Anyone Amy trusted, Kate felt she could more easily trust. They chatted for another two hours over a couple more beers. They finally called it a night when the mosquitoes became too intolerable.

"I'm going to look like a fifteen-year-old with severe acne if we stay sitting out here," Kevin said, standing and crushing his empty beer can.

"Same! I'm going to have to call the people who spray lawns to keep mosquitos away," Kate said laughing. "This is ridiculous! Anyway, have a good night, Kevin."

He smiled at her. "Goodnight, neighbor."

THAT NIGHT, Kate lay in bed staring at her ceiling. She had butterflies in her stomach and a smile on her face. Her mind was too wired to think about sleep. Was it Brian she was smiling over, or Kevin? Brian was tall, dark, and handsome, and Kevin was genuine and fun. Her alarm showed eleven o'clock when she rolled to her side and finally tried to close her eyes. A moment later, her phone sounded. She looked at it, and it said, "Motion detected. Front door."

What the hell, she thought as she opened the SimpliSafe app on her phone. As the camera loaded, her palms began to sweat. The leaves on the trees outside blew in the breeze, creating a soft white noise. She looked toward the window as the hair on her arms stood straight up, but she saw nothing. The recorded video finally loaded, and for a moment, she only saw the glow from her front porch lights and her steps leading down to her sidewalk. Then, a dark figure crossed her front doorbell. She couldn't make out what it was, but she immediately called Zan.

"What? What is it? Kate?" Zan said, sounding delirious, obviously just having woken up.

"There's something outside my house," Kate whispered, her voice trembling as she curled into a ball on top of her bed in full-panic mode.

"I'm on my way."

Zan woke up Amy and filled her in. She told her to stay home. Zan put on clothes, grabbed her firearm, and raced out the front door, setting her alarm as she went.

KATE REACHED under her bed where the gun safe was, pulling it up onto the bed. She pressed her finger on the sensor, and the cover unlocked. She flipped open the case and pulled out her 9mm Glock, thankful that she held full confidence in using it. Zan had trained her day after day until she felt comfortable.

A few minutes later, Zan pulled into Kate's driveway. She opened her door and pulled out her gun and flashlight. She pointed her flashlight up at Kate's window to signal she was there. Kate didn't move but saw the light and felt a pinch of relief. Zan walked around the left side of the house, looking for any signs of a person having been there. When she got around the perimeter, she'd determined no one was there. She went to Kate's front door and turned the knob. *Still locked, good,* she thought.

Kate's phone sounded again. "Motion detected. Front door." Her phone then started ringing. It was Zan. "Hey. I checked around your house. I'm at your front door." Kate, still holding her gun, ran downstairs and unlocked the door. She hugged Zan as tight as she could, thanking her endlessly for coming over.

She put down her gun and locked the door behind Zan, quickly resetting her alarm. They sat on the couch where Kate showed Zan the recording of the dark figure. "I don't know. I mean, it could have been a dog again. A big dog? No one is out there now."

"That's the second time this week," Kate said with wide eyes, sniffing her runny nose.

"Come on. You're coming to my house. You can sleep with Rocky," Zan demanded, knowing the dog would entice her more. She did not hesitate to go.

When they got back to Zan's place, Amy greeted them both with hugs. "Is everything okay?" she asked, concerned, looking into Zan's eyes for answers.

"It's ok. Kate is just going to sleep here tonight with Rocky," Zan told Amy.

After settling into the spare room, Kate slept on and off with Rocky at her feet. After hours of tossing and turning, she finally crawled out of bed when the sun rose in the morning.

16

MONDAY, JUNE 28, 2021

12:00 p.m.

Kate opened the store and worked the first four hours of the day, planning to hand it off to Ashley at noon. The bells on the door sounded, and Kate looked up to see Ashley coming in, noticing she still had her sunglasses on. Ashley walked straight to the back room, saying nothing as Alex drove off.

Smelling a hint of whiskey as Ashley walked by, Kate followed her to the back, knowing something was wrong. Ashley turned toward Kate and took off her sunglasses. "Okay. Before you say anything, I tried covering it with makeup, but it did no good." Ashley's left cheekbone was swollen. It almost looked like a golf ball was forming under her skin. Her eye was bloodshot. There was blue and purple bruising around her eye.

"What the hell happened?" Kate was suddenly horrified at what she saw, running to Ashley and putting her hand gently on Ashley's neck and face, examining her bruises.

"I had people over last night..." Ashley said, hesitating.

"Yeah?"

"We drank too much, and we were dancing in the kitchen when I slipped and fell. My face hit the corner of the counter. Like right on the edge! Seriously. It was so embarrassing!" Ashley admitted, barely making eye contact with Kate.

"Oh, honey. How do you feel? Do you have a concussion?" Kate asked, realizing she sounded like her mother.

"Oh no, I'm fine. Alex got me some frozen peas to put on it right away, and I fell asleep with them on my face. I showered, but sorry if I smell like peas," Ashley explained.

"Actually, I can smell whiskey more than I can smell peas," Kate sniffed toward Ashley. She stayed to make sure Ashley was okay. Having a challenging upbringing made Ashley into a tough girl. Kate had confidence in her when she said she was fine.

As Kate grabbed her purse to head home, the bells above the door chimed. In walked Brian.

"Hey, Kate. I was hoping to catch you. I was going to call, but I had to get a few things, so I figured I would just stop by and see if you were here," he said.

"Oh, hey. It's nice to see you again," Kate replied.

"Looks like you're heading out. Are you up for getting a drink later, or do you already have plans?"

Kate hesitated for a moment before agreeing, "Sure; no plans."

"Great. The Dugout, seven o'clock?" he asked with a smile.

"That works. See you there," Kate said, walking out the door, leaving Brian in the store with Ashley.

After oatmeal and an apple, Kate spent the rest of the afternoon outside mowing her lawn and planting flowers in a hanging pot on her porch. It was so hot that sweat-soaked her clothes, sticking to her skin. *I definitely need to shower before meeting Brian tonight,* she thought.

The cool water from the shower ran over Kate's body. She had set her alarm to "home" before going upstairs. This would alert her if any of her doors or windows opened while she was showering. Feeling safe and looking forward to the evening, she dried her hair and got ready for her date. Kate assumed a vintage charcoal gray dress with modest heels would match Brian's style.

She made the short walk to downtown Dover and headed into the bar. Brian was already there waiting for her. He handed her a light beer, and they walked over to a high-top table. "How did you know what kind of beer I drink?" Kate asked.

"You just seem like a light-beer type of girl," he replied, winking at her.

"Well, thank you," Kate replied.

"You're welcome."

To break the momentary silence, she asked, "So, how was your day? Did you work?"

"I did—just another day in the office. You know how it is," he replied.

She laughed. "In fact, I don't. I've been working at my mom's store since I was in high school. I've never had any other job."

"Sounds like a great job, though. I can't say you're missing too much working for someone else. I haven't met your mom yet, have I?" he asked.

Kate noticed he was finishing his first beer already. "You haven't. She passed away from cancer."

"I'm so sorry," he said. His brown eyes looked at her with concern.

An elderly couple walked by on their way out of the bar.

"Kate, I love what you've done with the front of the store this year. Your mother would be so proud, dear," the elderly woman said before squeezing her shoulder and continuing out of the bar.

"You seem to have a lot of support in town," Brian said.

"I do. Everyone has been so supportive. I feel like the whole town is my family. I love them all."

Brian stood, making it evident that he was finishing the last swig of his beer. "Would you like another?"

"I'm okay, thank you."

A few minutes later, Brian returned with another beer for himself. Kate noticed him moving awkwardly around chairs in the bar to get back to their table. He motioned to sit, pushing the chair a few inches backward, and it almost came out from underneath him.

Kate couldn't help but ask, "Did you have a shot up there without me?"

He eyed her and gave a sarcastic laugh even though she wasn't joking with her question. "I had a couple of drinks with lunch today."

Not caring if she sounded rude, she replied, "Sorry I missed the party." By this point, she wished she had just let him get her another drink. The bartender looked at Kate and held up a beer, pointing at it asking if she wanted another. She nodded that she did.

"So, what do you do for work again?"

"Business. Companies hire me for contract to run internal investigations and audits. Really, it's nothing exciting," he replied, clearly wanting to change the subject, she guessed, by the lack of depth he gave her.

"Ever found anything fraudulent?" she asked.

"Of course. All of the time. It's just a matter of *how* fraud-ulent and what the company wants to do with the information I give them." He was so nonspecific yet professional in his answers.

After Kate's second beer, she hinted she was ready to leave. Brian paid the tab, and they headed out the front door.

"Thank you for the drinks," Kate said.

"You're welcome. Do you want a ride home?" Brian asked.

"Sure," she said, even though she lived so close.

Brian opened the passenger door for Kate then went around to the driver's side to get in. It was such a short ride that they didn't say a word on the way. Upon arriving, Kate got out of the car, assuming he would follow. As he did, she met him at the front of his car and gave him a quick, light hug.

"Thanks again," she said.

"Maybe see you again sometime?" he asked.

"Maybe," Kate said.

Little did Kate know, as Brian was pulling away, he was thinking to himself, *I have to get her to trust me.*

17

TUESDAY, JUNE 29, 2021

7:50 a.m.

Kate unlocked the door to Julie's and made her way inside. The breeze from outside flooded in when the door opened, making Kate's dress fly up in all directions. She saw something flutter around near the register when the door shut behind her. Something typically so small, she wouldn't think twice about it. But this was so brilliantly white. She had a gut feeling she should figure out what it was.

Kate looked down but couldn't decipher what the object was until she got on the ground, on her hands and knees, and looked under the shelf. There it was. She reached out and picked it up. It was soft, white, and delicate. It was a white rose petal. *Where did this come from?* She thought. She certainly didn't carry white roses in her store, nor did she have any as decorations out front, only lilies. There was a time when she was young that she found a white rose dried in the pages of a thick book her mother kept at her bedside. Because of the memories of her mother and what she thought could be a good luck charm, Kate took the rose petal into the back room of the store, where she put it on the shelf of her locker.

She restocked the paint samples and straightened up the racks, waiting for her first customer. Brian came across her mind when she was in the paint area, and Kevin when she straightened the books.

After an hour, the front door opened, and in walked Amy. "Hey! How are you?"

"I'm fine. Went on another date last night with Brian."

"Oh, yeah? How was that?"

"It was a decent date," she said, "but I was ready for it to be done."

"How come?" Amy asked, grabbing a few Fourth of July decorations off the shelf.

"Eh, I don't know. He's really nice and charming, but he kind of drinks too much," Kate admitted.

"Yeah, well, don't we all?" Amy asked, trying to make light of the situation. "Did you, by chance, get those flags in yet?" She was referring to the rainbow flags she had Kate order.

"Yeah, I did. I have them back here," she said, walking to the back room to grab them.

"Amazing. Thank you!" Amy said to her. They already had a flagpole posted; they just needed the flag. Kate handed it to her and set out another one for herself.

"Of course," Kate replied.

They turned to walk back to the front of the store when Amy glimpsed at something in Kate's still-open locker. She was curious so she backpedaled, approaching Kate's locker to pick up what she saw. It was the white rose petal. "Kate. Where did you get this?"

"What?" she asked, turning around walking back toward Amy.

"This," Amy said, showing Kate the rose petal.

"It was on the floor. When I came into the store this morning, it must have blown inside. I thought it might be my good luck charm. Mom had a white rose dried in a book she kept on her nightstand that she got from my dad, I guess, so I thought it was a sign from her."

"Kate..." Amy started.

She filled Kate in on the evidence found at Stacie's and Amber's home. "The rapes are likely related, Kate. There is a dangerous person out there. I mean, maybe this just blew in from on the street, but what if it didn't? What if the murderer was in your store?"

Kate grew pale. She felt nauseous and suddenly terrified.

18

Nate walked all day until his thirst was too intense to keep ignoring. He saw a gas station in the distance and headed in its direction. A few dollars from his piggy bank had been stuffed in his pockets before he left, so he went inside to buy a Gatorade.

"Hey, bud. Aren't you supposed to be in school?" the cashier asked. He was a skinny young man with long, straight blonde hair leaning against the counter, looking down at Nate.

"Yeah, my mom is out in the car. We had to go to an appointment, but I'm going back to school now," he lied.

"Here's your change. See ya next time," the cashier said.

"See ya," Nate replied, sounding casual.

Another hour into his walk, Nate came across a large farm. There was a brand-new appearing red barn. It was the biggest he'd ever seen, and a two-story white house only fifty yards away. He noticed an old shed that looked like it could fall with one strong gust of wind, and a frail old barn that looked as though it had been damaged in a tornado. That, or time was causing it to fall apart. Half of the roof was missing, along with random boards on the west side of it. It was clearly not being used, so he walked toward it. Upon entering the old, broken barn, he saw a pile of hay in the corner surrounded by cobwebs and empty, rusty pails. It was good enough to be his shelter for the night, he decided.

The barn was far enough away from the farmhouse that Nate felt comfortable settling in. He had brought a coloring book and a few children's books to look through. They were items he used to pass the time while hiding in his room. The sun had descended enough that he could no longer see the pages, so he pulled out his blanket and covered himself, trying to find comfort in the small pile of hay.

Coyotes cried in the woods nearby. Inside, the barn had become nearly black. The moon and stars provided the only light Nate would see that night, but he was okay with that. The stars were so beautiful, and Nate was not being yelled at or abused. He closed his eyes as the loneliness set in. He'd always felt alone at home, but now he was at least safe from Chuck.

HUNGRY COWS CALLING to the farmer woke Nate just as the sun was rising. He laid there for a while, enjoying the peace, trying to figure out a plan for the day. He knew he'd have to keep going so the farmers wouldn't find him in the barn.

He saw a semi-trailer full of corn and knew it would need to go to Winona to be put on a barge and shipped elsewhere. A ladder extended from the bottom of the semi to the top, leading to the corn. *Maybe I could hide in there*, he thought. But then he remembered how easy it was for people to get sucked down into corn. It happened a few times when farmers got lost within the corn in tall silver silos. The fire department had to cut sections of the silo off, clearing small amounts of corn at a time, hoping to find the body to be taken to the funeral home.

The cab. Nate considered. The cab of the semi would have a sleeping area. If he could somehow get himself in there to ride to the river and sneak his way out, he'd be even further from home and sustaining his freedom.

Nate took a drink of Gatorade and ate a granola bar he'd put in his backpack, along with a few other snacks. He tightened the straps of his backpack around his shoulders and peeked out the lopsided entrance of the old wooden barn, a move he was used to doing. No one was around. He assumed the farmer was feeding the cows now, considering they all migrated to one corner of the fence near the modern barn. Taking a leap of faith, Nate stayed low to the ground and ran toward the semi-truck. Once he reached it, he hid underneath to catch his breath and reassess his surroundings.

The front porch door opened, and Nate saw two legs wearing jeans and old tennis shoes descend the stairs and head toward the cows. As the robust woman went further away from the semi, Nate planned his next move. She rounded the corner and walked out of sight into the barn presenting the perfect opportunity for Nate to hop into the cab of the truck. He inched out from under the semi and crawled up the side, barely reaching the handle. He gave it a good tug and opened the door. He crawled inside and looked toward the barn to be sure no one was coming. They weren't. Nate gently closed the door, but it still made a loud thud as it locked into place. He froze. But still, he saw nothing coming from the barn and no one else around. He crawled around to the back of the cab and sat cross-legged, catching his breath. *I did it,* he thought to himself. This gave him the confidence to keep going.

THE MISSISSIPPI RIVER separates southern Minnesota and Wisconsin. The truck driver had his window down, and Nate was able to hear them transfer the corn from the semitrucks onto the barges, the geese flying above, and the sound of the water as it crashed against the boats.

There were multiple trucks and people around, so he had to be careful. The driver got out of the truck when he'd reached his destination, and Nate peeked around the corner to see if he was far enough away that he could sneak out. He was, so Nate left. He crawled across the seat, opened the door, and hopped onto the gravel road, closing the door behind him.

He looked around and made a run for the trees off to the left, near the river. He ran as fast as he could, unsure if anyone was watching. His backpack was bouncing as he zigzagged around trees, through swampy water, over fallen branches, and further from the semi. He didn't want to turn around to look just in case anyone was following. Nate found his way to a clearing in the trees that led to the river but didn't expect there would be people there. He froze like a deer in headlights.

The people were sitting in old broken chairs around a campfire, though there was no fire burning. He saw the first man with long shaggy hair and a long beard, wearing an old shirt and shorts. He then saw a woman at the tree line with her hair in a bun, hanging clothes on a string that went from one tree to the next. It didn't look like they were camping; it looked like they lived there.

"Hey, boy," a man behind Nate said, startling him. Nate stumbled forward, nearly landing on his face.

"What are you doing here, boy?" the man asked.

"I... I... I was just looking for somewhere to hang out for a bit. My parents went out of town, and I got bored, so I wandered here from the city. I wanted to see the river," Nate said, stumbling over the words as he made up the story on the fly.

"Alright then. I have an extra chair. Come, have a seat," the man said. Let me show you around our tent city.

19

TUESDAY, JUNE 29, 2021

12:45 p.m.

Zan came into the store heading straight for the back room with an evidence bag. Kate sat in a nearby chair, still looking pale, as Amy showed her the rose petal. They used tweezers to pick up the petal and place it into the bag. Zan sealed the top, and they all stared at it for a moment like it was haunted. Nancy showed up to run the store while Kate sat frazzled in the back with Amy at her side.

She was quietly sitting, staring straight ahead. She wiped a tear off her cheek with the back of her hand and asked, "What do I do now?"

"You carry your gun with you," Zan replied. "And your cat ears. And your pepper spray. You have cameras in your store, right? Do they record everything?"

"I can only see the live feed. It doesn't record," Kate replied.

"Damn. I was hoping we could look to see who was in your store yesterday," Zan said, disheartened but eager for more answers. "Maybe you should figure out how to get it to record from here on out."

"I've been trying to recollect everyone that's come in. I had a ton of customers. There's no way I'd be able to keep track of everyone," Kate said, disappointed and concerned.

"Alright, well, how about anyone you didn't know?"

"Not that I remember, but I wasn't here the whole time, either. Ashley was here when I went on a date with Brian," Kate replied. She halted and gasped, putting her hand to her chest. "Brian was in the store, Zan. No one knows Brian. He's new to town. But it couldn't have been him. Could it have been? Was it him? If he wanted to hurt me, he could have. But he didn't." She was frantic.

"Wait, wait. The guy you went on a date with?" Zan questioned.

"Yes!"

"Most victims of sexual assault know their attacker. But not all. I'm going to call McGriff. We'll check surveillance videos from other stores that may show us everyone who came in this weekend," Zan assured her. She was intelligent, calm, and Kate felt safe with her being there. She turned and went into the main part of the store, pulling out her phone to call Deputy McGriff.

"Hey, McGriff. Zan here. You gotta get down to Julie's. There's something you need to see."

Douglas McGriff arrived within minutes. He and Zan went around to the other businesses to review video footage while Kate went back out into the store to relieve Nancy.

"Oh, honey. I'm not going anywhere," Nancy said.

"You came in on your day off. You don't need to stay, Nance," Kate said, encouraging her to leave. Julie always called Nancy "Nance." It was something Kate picked up on at a young age.

"Well, I am," Nancy replied. Kate knew not to argue. She would not change her mind.

KATE AND NANCY were getting ready to close for the night when Zan came back. She filled Kate in on what they found on video surveillance from other businesses. Or rather, what they didn't find.

"We didn't see anything unusual," Zan said. "The only one that records everything is the camera outside of The Dugout. We saw people coming in and out, but none of them were carrying a white rose. We saw Brian come in, but he wasn't carrying anything either. Alex picked up Ashley at the end of the night, and there was nothing out of the norm that we noticed there either. We're sending the footage to the station to be reviewed in more detail by the team. I'll let you know if anything else comes about from it."

Zan drove Kate to her house and walked her in. "I'm fine, Zan. I have my gun, pepper spray, and alarm system. I'll know if anything suspicious is going on." Kate was already pouring herself a glass of red wine at the kitchen counter by the time she finished her sentence.

"Okay. Call me if you need anything. My phone stays on loud for you, girl," Zan replied before heading out the front door. "Oh, lock this behind me, will ya?"

Kate didn't reply. All she did was hold up her glass of wine and nod at Zan. *You got it, boss,* she thought.

Smart lock engaged, alarm system set, front porch lights on. Kate took her glass of wine and stood in the entryway of her living room. She stared at the floor but couldn't move any further. She realized she was alone and that she may have encountered a murderer. The white rose found in her store paralyzed her with fear. Maybe it was a fluke. Maybe it was the murderer. Maybe this is all a nightmare. *Is this real life?* She questioned.

While staring at nothing, unable to feel her arms and legs, Kate's phone vibrated from an incoming text message. She snapped out of the daze and pulled her phone out of her pocket: *Message from Brian.*

Unlocking her phone and opening the message, it read: *Hey, I had a great time last night, but things ended a little odd. Interested in getting coffee tomorrow?*

She locked her phone again and put it back in her pocket. There were more important decisions to make right now and replying to a potential murderer was not one of them. There were panic buttons strategically placed around her home, in addition to the window sensors, door sensors, smart locks, doorbell camera, three other strategically placed cameras, motion sensor, and the glass-break sensor. If anyone entered, Kate would know. But even if someone did enter, they'd still have time to find Kate before police would get there. She had to take extra precautions.

Kate went upstairs to change into pajamas. She took the gun out of the safe under her bed and loaded it, putting it in her robe pocket. Back downstairs, she set pepper spray on the coffee table, along with the cat ears before curling up in her chair to watch Netflix and try to relax.

HOURS LATER, an alert from Kate's phone woke her suddenly from her light slumber in the recliner. She sat up and grabbed her phone. It was nearly midnight. "Motion detected. Front door." Panic set in her chest, triggering the adrenaline to course through her body. She hadn't meant to fall asleep in the chair, but now she was wide awake. Her stomach sank to the floor as she opened her alarm system app to view the recording from the doorbell.

A dark figure walked across the sidewalk leading to her front door and kept walking across the other side of her yard. All she could see was a person in a dark sweater with a hood up and dark pants. This time, she could tell it was a person.

Fuck! she thought.

Her alarm system wasn't going off, so she knew he wasn't in the house. Slowly leaning forward to crawl out of the recliner, the floor creaked as her weight shifted. She was twenty feet from the staircase that led to the master bedroom upstairs. Staying low to the ground, she made her way over. Once she got there, she bolted up the steps and into her bedroom, closing and locking the door behind her.

Kate gripped the gun in her palm. A bang came from the front of her house, and she jumped, catching herself before she screamed. She inched to the window and looked down to where the porch lights lit up the ground and nearly the entire front of her house.

There he was.

It was a man in a dark sweater and dark pants, crouched by the side of her porch. *What the hell is he doing?* she thought. After a moment of staring at the man, she recognized the neon orange tennis shoes.

It's Kevin.

Still holding her gun, Kate took out her phone and opened her alarm app, shutting off her alarm system so she could open her window. She set down her phone, keeping her gun in one hand as she opened the window. Looking down, she yelled through the screen, "What the hell are you doing?"

Kevin startled. He stopped what he was doing but didn't

move for a moment. He slowly turned around and looked up at Kate's window, only seeing darkness. "Uh... Hey, Kate."

"What the hell! I'm going to call the cops if you don't tell me what the hell you're doing!"

"I'm so sorry, you weren't supposed to hear me," Kevin called up to her. He turned back around to what he was doing, ignoring her question.

"Kevin, I'm serious. I'm calling the cops!" Kate yelled.

Still looking toward the ground, he said, "Just a minute."

Only a few seconds later, her porch brightened. Beautiful cream lights glowed, swirling around the railing of her porch and up the support beams. Both sides lit up, and it was breathtaking.

"When I went to your store the other day, a lady working there was talking with another lady about your upcoming birthday. I wasn't trying to eavesdrop. It just happened. She mentioned how you and your mom planted the lilies in front of the store on your birthday." He paused before continuing, "You weren't supposed to wake up. I suppose I scared the hell out of you."

"You're goddamn right you did." Kate hesitated for a moment, unsure of what to do. Should she trust him? She contemplated but thought of the kindness Kevin had shown her every time they've seen each other. She also thought of the friendship he and Amy had. Kate finally said, "I'll be right down."

She had an anxious feeling in her stomach. Was it because she felt terrified, or were the lights just so beautiful? Was she happy to see Kevin because this was the most beautiful and thoughtful gift she'd ever received?

Kate strapped her belly band around her waist under her robe and put her gun in the holster. Her big robe hid it well. She put on her slippers and made her way down the stairs. She hesitated for a moment before unlocking her front door. *Is this safe? What if... no... I have my gun...* she debated before opening the front door.

When the door opened, she couldn't step out. Her front porch was the sight she'd always wanted—a true vision. All around her, the lights glowed. There were fake white lilies strategically placed within the lights on the banister, her mother's favorite flower.

"Kevin..." she lost her words. Any thought that led her to believe Kevin was a murderer completely vanished from her mind after opening the door. "This is absolutely beautiful."

He let her take in the scene, watching her eyes light up. "I'm glad you like it."

"It's perfect." She stepped onto her porch and touched the lights as though they were magic. She smiled as though she was seeing the sun for the first time in years before settling her eyes on Kevin.

"I don't know how to thank you," Kate told him.

"Please don't. I'm sure I'll need a cup of sugar, or a beer, or something now that we're neighbors."

Kate sat on the step, and they chatted for a few minutes. "You know, I'm curious about one thing," Kate said.

"What's that?"

"Your tattoo."

"Ah," Kevin said. "My lion?"

Kevin touched the scar on his forehead and said, "I had a brother. He was two years younger. I was his protector, ya know?" He paused for a moment, staring into the darkness before continuing, "He was so smart. He always called himself the owl because I'd never let him forget how smart he was. I was the lion, supposedly the brave and courageous one."

Kevin put his hand on his arm where his sweatshirt

covered his tattoo and went on, "Matt died in Afghanistan last year. I was over there with him. I was supposed to be protecting him. I got the tattoo so I could always remember how he saw me." Kevin lifted his sweatshirt, revealing the owl tattoo on his chest over his heart, "And he'll always be an owl to me."

"I'm so sorry, Kevin," Kate replied, unsure of what else to say.

"No, I'm sorry. Really, you weren't supposed to hear me," he said apologetically.

"I'm glad I did," she said, smiling a little as her fears dissipated.

"Happy early birthday, Kate."

20

WEDNESDAY, JUNE 30, 2021

7:35 a.m.

The sound of a car pulling into her driveway gave Kate motivation to get out of bed. She was lying there, enjoying the morning sun and trying to process what happened yesterday. The aroma from her timer-set coffee downstairs willed her to get up. Peering out her window, she acknowledged that the porch lights shut off at 7:00 a.m., so they were no longer glowing, but it was still a beautiful sight. Then she saw Alex's rusty old car. He and Ashley got out and walked up the sidewalk to Kate's front door.

The blue robe covered Kate again as she descended the stairs. Before they could ring the doorbell, Kate opened the door. "Isn't it a little early to stop by?" she asked quizzically.

"Alex said he saw a couple of police cars in front of Julie's yesterday. I wanted to make sure you were okay," Ashley said.

"You couldn't have called?" Kate replied, giving her a *you're-in-trouble-young-lady* look. "I text you, you know."

Ashley hesitated and looked down at her feet. "My phone is broken."

"She thought it was a good idea to put it on the roof of the car, and it flew off. By the time we found it, someone had run it over. Maybe a couple of times, by the looks of it," Alex added.

"I'll have to get a new one next time I go into town," Ashley finished.

"Ah. Well yeah, everything is fine. Just some weird things happening, is all. We can talk about it later. I'll come by the store after a bit," Kate said.

"Ok. I'm glad you're okay. Love the extra bling you have on your porch! And the lilies, those are a nice touch." Ashley said, hugging Kate.

"Birthday gift from the neighbor, believe it or not."

"Wow, lucky you! You'll have to tell me about that later, too. Happy early birthday, Kate. Love you," Ashley said as she turned to head back down the porch steps.

"Thank you. Love you," Kate replied.

"See ya later, Kate," Alex said, escorting Ashley back to the car. He no longer looked like a prom date, but back to looking like a poor jock. His clothes were old, and his car matched. *Maybe I should go get her damn car myself,* Kate thought.

MEANWHILE, Zan and Douglas were told investigators finally had a lead on the murderer. They requested to interview a neighbor of the victim and had a few interesting things to say.

"I got up to go to the bathroom like I do every night, but then I heard a car. I thought it was pretty late for people to be driving around the neighborhood, so I looked out and saw a gray car go by," the elderly woman said, shaking her head with sorrow. She explained she didn't recognize the car, nor did she hear it drive by again.

"Thank you so much for your time, ma'am. Is there anything else before we go?" Zan asked.

"Yeah. When I was getting my perm down at the salon, I heard some ladies talking about the girl who was raped a couple of months back. Supposedly she's a niece to one lady who comes in for a lip wax every month. They said the girl was Amber Stray. I eavesdropped a little harder after that because I recognized the name. Amber Stray was a good friend of Stacie. If you didn't know any better, you'd think they were sisters," she said, looking up at McGriff.

Amber, the first victim, was good friends with Stacie, the second victim. They knew each other, Zan thought as the lady spoke. More pieces were falling together; the world was becoming smaller, and she felt one small step closer to narrowing in on the murderer.

KATE STILL HADN'T RESPONDED to Brian. Instead, she went downstairs for a cup of coffee. The sun was up, and it was already sixty-five degrees Fahrenheit outside, a perfect summer morning to have coffee and paint.

After an hour, Kate felt zoned into what she was doing. Hearing cars drive by her house was not unusual, but she turned around when she heard a car come to a stop. Paintbrush in hand, she turned to look.

It was Brian. *Fuck.*

Not knowing what to do, she put her hands in her robe pockets where she kept her cat ears and stood up, facing Brian's car.

"Kate, hey! I'm sorry for showing up like this. I went to

St. Charles to grab some coffee and a doughnut, and I got two in case I might see you out here," Brian said kindly.

"Ah, I have coffee. Thank you, though," Kate replied, holding up her cup, trying to sound calm and collected yet uninviting.

"But you don't have Cabin Coffee coffee!" he teased. Brian made his way up to Kate's sidewalk with two cups of coffee and a small bag in his hands. "I hope I didn't upset you, Kate. I'm sorry. I'm really not good at this whole dating thing. Truthfully, I wasn't sure I was ready to date again until I saw you in your store. I couldn't help but ask you out when we ran into each other. My wife and I split up six months ago. I needed a change. That's part of the reason I came here. Maybe I'm not as ready as I thought I was. I've been letting beer and whiskey control me a little bit too much lately. It's been my vice to help me forget about her," he said.

"I'm sorry about your split," Kate said, momentarily forgetting he could be a murderer.

"Nah, that's okay. Anyway, here," he said, handing her the coffee and the bag with a doughnut inside. "Friends?"

"Alright. Friends," Kate agreed, slipping her right hand out of her robe pocket, releasing the death grip she had on her cat ears. She was glad he decided for the two of them only to be friends. It saved her from having to come up with something on the fly about why she hadn't responded to his message. He likely knew the reason, anyway. But still, she didn't approve of him randomly showing up at her house.

"Your porch looks great! New lights?" he asked.

"Yep. A birthday gift, actually," Kate replied.

"That's an amazing gift. Wow. You have great support, Kate," Brian said. They talked for a short bit until he said he had to go to work. Mixed emotions came over Kate as he left. It was nice to have made a new friend who was charming and confident, but at the same time, she was relieved that the potential murderer had left her house.

Hey. The Island? Kate texted Amy.

The Island. 15 minutes, Amy replied.

The Island was a chunk of land protruding into the middle of the creek just outside of town. It was twenty years ago that The Island got its name. Amy and Kate were fishing in the creek one afternoon after record rainfall. As naive children, they thought more fish would go down the creek since the current was faster. They didn't realize that while the water was flowing faster, it was also eating away at the land.

Standing at the edge of The Island casting her fishing pole, the dirt under Amy's feet suddenly gave way, and she fell into the creek. She was immediately sucked underwater. Kate screamed for Amy. She followed the current and finally saw Amy emerge from the water fifty yards down before yelling, "Kate!" and going under again.

Twenty yards further was a fallen tree in the water. Amy was bobbing up and down, riding the current, trying to keep her head above water. Kate yelled for Amy to go toward the tree, hoping she could reach out for it. The rushing waters brought her inches from the tree, but she reached out and was able to grab a branch. She held on for her life. Amy pulled herself further up the fallen tree toward the creek bank as the branch she was holding cracked. One more crack and the branch broke, dangling by only a thread.

"Amy! Hold on!" Kate yelled.

Kate reached out her arm as far as she could, holding onto the trunk of the tree when finally they were able to grab ahold of each other. With all the strength she had, Kate pulled Amy in. They both fell on the ground, rolling to their backs. Amy was coughing up water while Kate was breathing heavily as though she'd just run a marathon. They lay there until they could catch their breath.

A few minutes later, Amy finally spoke, "Thanks for saving me, Kate."

"Hey, Amy?" Kate replied.

"Yeah?"

"You lost a shoe." They both burst out laughing, forgetting Amy had almost been washed away with the current like a broken tree branch. When they finally got up and walked back to their fishing spot, they looked at each other and said, "Fucking island." And since, they've been calling it The Island.

Whenever they said this name, the other knew it was an emergent situation, and they had to meet.

AFTER FIFTEEN MINUTES on the dot, Amy walked up to Kate sitting by the creek. "What's up, Buttercup?" she asked.

When Kate turned around, Amy knew something was wrong. Kate broke down and admitted her anxiety about everything that had been happening over the last couple of days. The white rose petal, Brian and their most recent date, Kevin and his middle-of-the-night visit to her house.

"Wow," was all Amy could say.

"I know. I mean, what's been freaking me out the most is the rose petal. Could it be a coincidence?"

"I don't know, sweetie. I hope they catch that fucker. Maybe you should close your store for a few days?" Amy asked.

"I can't do that. What if they never catch the guy? My mom never closed the store the entire time it's been open.

I'm not about to do it now because a damn flower petal was on the floor," Kate replied, angry at the situation. "I have my cameras set to record now. I should have done that from the start, but it's Dover, for Christ's sake. I didn't think I would need that."

"I still think you should consider. Do you know what Zan told me on my way here? The two victims knew each other. They were friends. Why would the guy go after two women who were friends? Because they were on to him? Because he had something against them? Maybe he knew them," Amy told Kate.

"Jesus," Kate replied, staring into the water.

Amy and Kate sat on the creek bank for a bit, not saying anything. Instead, they soaked up the rays from the sun, contemplating the possibilities of why the petal was in Kate's store and if it meant something.

AN HOUR LATER, a server brought two buffalo chicken salads out to Kate and Amy at The Dugout. Kate had asked how the Twins game went and listened to Amy rave about the experience. She watched Amy talk and tried hard to concentrate, but her mind kept wandering. Thankfully, she could nod and agree like she'd been following along with complete focus.

"They look like me," Kate said out of nowhere.

"Huh?" Amy replied.

"The girl who was raped and the girl who was murdered. They both look like me: long brown hair, big brown eyes. I looked them up on social media to see if I recognized them," she explained.

"That's coincidence, love."

"I hope so."

21

SUMMER 1997

Ten months of living in the tent city had been a godsend for Nate. After three days, the man figured out Nate's parents weren't simply out of town. The way Nate trembled when he went near him, his fear of being heard and seen, and the pain in his eyes were dead giveaways. But in addition to the pain in his eyes, there was also something dark and cold.

The man, Ross, and his informal wife, Kya, took in Nate as one of their own. Because of how long they'd been living in their community, they were well past the idea of normalcy and democracy. They had established their own loose version of family and government.

After only a few days, Nate broke down to Ross and Kya about his past, leaving them with a passion for keeping him safe. He was learning English, science, and math with a few other children who lived in the tent city, though they were fifteen and sixteen years old. Nate was a brilliant child, but he often became distracted by deep anger they couldn't understand.

22

Wednesday, June 30, 2021

5:00 p.m.

Kate went to the store to relieve Ashley. She came through the door cautiously, investigating the floor for anything unusual. She looked around but saw nothing. Ashley was busy with a customer when Kate came in, so she went straight to the back to put away her purse.

"Thank you! Have a great day!" Ashley said as the customer left. "Hey, Kate."

"Hey Ash," Kate replied. She took over Ashley's shift in running the store, but Ashley wasn't in a hurry to leave. It was unusual because Alex had been coming at her shift-end time on the dot for the last two weeks, if not early. "Alex coming?" Kate asked.

"I don't know. Hopefully not. I told him I was going to walk home," Ashley said.

"Five miles? Why?"

"He was a jerk. I'm just taking my time, I guess."

"Stay as long as you like, dear," Kate offered.

But only a few minutes later, Alex pulled up in front of

the store. Ashley noticed but didn't go outside. She wondered how long he'd wait or if he'd come into the store. Ashley made herself busy straightening the books and magazines as Alex walked in. He quietly approached her. He put his arms around her waist and hugged her from behind, glancing at Kate as he did.

"I'm sorry, baby," he whispered into her ear, leaning around and kissing her neck. But she didn't reply. She tried to keep organizing the books, blowing him off. "Can I take you home?" he asked.

Again, she didn't reply.

"Ashley, I'm sorry. Let me take you home."

"Fine," she gave in. She eyed Kate and said, "See ya later, Kate."

Kate wasn't sure if she should say something or intervene. Unsure of what else to do, she tried to sound calm when she said, "Bye, Ashley."

Ashley gave a small smile then turned to walk out of the store with Alex.

McGriff and Ramiro assisted the primary investigators on the case by visiting with Stacie's mom, expressing condolences and interviewing her at the same time.

"They've been friends for years. Amber was a year older than Stacie, but that didn't stop them from being best friends. I just don't understand. I don't understand why someone would hurt the two of them. You're sure it was the same person?" she asked.

"That's what we're trying to figure out, ma'am," Deputy McGriff said. "And yes, it seems as though it was the same person for both situations." As he was talking, Ramiro eyed the room and glanced at some photos on a poster board they must have displayed at Stacie's funeral. There was another brunette girl in many of the photos with Stacie. Ramiro got up to look closer, noticing that the two girls looked very similar, though one was shorter and thinner than the other. Long brown hair, dark eyes, minimal makeup, yet beautiful. It was Amber and Stacie.

"They look so similar," Ramiro said to herself, accidentally loud enough for Stacie's mom to hear.

"They do. People always thought they were sisters," she said.

"And what about Stacie's father? Has he been in the picture?" Zan questioned.

"No. Never. He knocked me up and was out the door only weeks after I had Stacie. He'd been sober when I met him and swore he'd change. He didn't," she said and suddenly became emotional. Ramiro could see the tears well in her eyes, spilling over the brim and down her face. "I didn't even put his name on her birth certificate. He's worthless. Please, I just want to find my daughter's killer. Please find him," she begged.

"We're going to do everything we can, ma'am," McGriff replied.

Stacie's mom nodded then stood. "If you don't mind, I have some friends coming by shortly. It was nice to meet you both," she said, ending the visit.

They went back to the squad car and headed back to the station. "Did you see how much those girls look alike?" Ramiro asked.

"I did. I never noticed it before until there was a picture of them right next to each other. Maybe that's his type? We should look into more friends of theirs. Maybe one of their guy friends? Let's touch base with the guys working on this case then go through their social media and mutual friends lists," McGriff replied.

"That's exactly what I was thinking," said Ramiro.

THEY PULLED UP THE GIRLS' social media back at the station, listing out mutual friends on the whiteboard, paying attention to where the guys lived and their age. "Twenty mutual friends," McGriff stated, finalizing their search.

"Sounds like we better get started," Ramiro replied.

Amber's rape kit had finally come back with results. While it showed male DNA from her kit, there were no matches after running it through the database. They'd have to collect DNA and alibis from the twenty men. Knowing there wasn't any time to waste, the deputies kept working.

One by one, they found addresses for each of the guys. Their locations ranged from Dover to Seattle, Washington, and New York City. They'd have to see if any of the men flew home in the last few months—an easy way to rule out the men who were far away. By eleven o'clock at night, they came up with a plan for who to interview and collect DNA from first. "See you at seven sharp, McGriff," Ramiro said, walking to her car.

"Six-fifty-nine," McGriff replied.

23

FALL 1997

Nate had been gone for a year. Despite wondering if Chuck had killed her son, Natalie didn't give up hope that he would one day find his way back to her. For the first few months, her drug use had been at an all-time high. She couldn't deal with the fact that Nate was no longer with her. It wasn't until the Christmas after Nate left that her drug use stopped altogether. Instead of hiding from her intense pain of losing Nate, Christmas morning came, and she knew she needed to do something about it. She hated Chuck. He was the reason Nate left or the reason he was dead.

IN EARLY JANUARY OF 1998, Natalie went to the police station to report domestic abuse. They took photographs of the bruises on her arms and around her neck. Chuck was a name they were familiar with at the station, so they assisted Natalie in evicting him from her home. She got a restraining order, leaving her alone in her trailer, sober, mapping out every direction Nate could have gone.

Being sober was an unfamiliar experience for Natalie. It was something she had felt for only a day or two at a time since Nate was young, but now she saw a clarity that was so beautiful. It was life. It was choice. It was overcoming. It was horror at the fact that she could have prevented her son from running away. While she blamed Chuck, she also blamed herself. She should have been stronger for Nate. If only.

While being sober made her face her feelings head-on, it also put her in a better position to strategize how to get Nate back. She wrote down all their family in the area and every friend she could think of whom Nate would have known. *Maybe he's hiding in plain sight, living with someone, keeping him safe from Chuck,* she thought.

CHUCK HAD NOWHERE TO GO. He'd burned all bridges he had because of drugs, alcohol, and his temper. He somehow sweet-talked one of his ex-girlfriends into letting him stay with her, pretending to love her and pretending he missed her the whole time they'd been apart. But truthfully, he picked this ex-girlfriend because she was the only one he hadn't had a child with. He didn't want to deal with children anymore. They were a burden, and he knew Nate was the reason Natalie kicked him out. He didn't consider the fact that it was his abuse, keeping her hooked on drugs and alcohol, controlling everything she did, every penny she made, and all the air she breathed. He hated Nate since he met him, as he did with any child, but that hate grew even more intense since he'd been kicked out of Natalie's to the streets.

. . .

CHUCK HAD HIS FIRST BABY—A little girl—before he got hooked on drugs. It was the best relationship he had because it was the only one he was sober for. Unfortunately, parenting had never been for him. He didn't want children. The crying, diapers, bottles, and vomit all pushed him over the edge, and he left.

What he didn't learn, though, was the art of using protection. He'd gotten another woman pregnant after he'd been well into drugs. She was hooked on drugs, too, having no idea she was pregnant until she was seven months along and realized she hadn't been gaining weight from food, but because of the child growing in her body. Unfortunately, the baby was hooked on drugs, too.

Before she gave birth, Chuck was gone. Born six weeks early, the child was given up for adoption after it was weaned off drugs. Those beautiful brown eyes had gotten her adopted by a male couple unable to have children of their own.

And Chuck's final child was born only one year later, a third little girl. A little girl born into an unfortunate situation but thankfully not hooked on drugs.

Chuck was fixated on the woman's long brown hair and dark eyes, but because she'd been in a previous abusive relationship, she kicked Chuck out as soon as his angry side showed. The baby's mother had kept her, unable to give up the darling child she'd been longing to have. She named her Stacie.

24

8:45 a.m.

"We'll need to see your receipts, sir," Ramiro asked in a stern voice. They were interviewing their third suspect on the list. The first two willingly gave DNA samples knowing what had happened to their friends. They also had tight alibis. The third, though, did not.

"I mean, I probably don't have them. Who keeps receipts?" he said, sounding eager to express his innocence but fumbling over his words.

"How about your email? Did you get a confirmation email when you bought the tickets?" she asked.

"Oh! Yeah, yeah! I got that right here," he said, excited for a win. He pulled up his confirmation email and offered to forward it to them.

"Great. Can you get us a copy of your bank statements? If there are charges on your cards from Texas, we'll know you actually got on that plane," McGriff added.

The man anxiously agreed to get bank statements. He

hadn't been close with Amber or Stacie, but he'd known them through a mutual friend.

McGriff and Ramiro moved on to the next house for the fourth interview. They didn't call the suspects to give them a heads-up but showed up unannounced, so there would be no time to plan an alibi or plan for the interview. Or destroy evidence.

By five-thirty, they'd made it through twelve of the suspects. They took five off the suspect list but still collected DNA. The other seven needed to prove their whereabouts on the night of Amber's rape and Stacie's murder. If the murderer were one of these seven men, he would be a flight risk. There was nothing more they could do at the time to keep them in custody.

KEVIN PULLED into his gravel driveway, the rocks crunching under his truck. He admired his handy work on Kate's porch, at the same time still feeling bad for scaring her.

Kate washed her dishes, peering out the window that showed her a perfect view of Kevin's driveway and house. She and Amy were going to The Dugout at six for some drinks and appetizers for her birthday, hoping Zan would come after work. She didn't want anything fancy. She didn't want to dress up or go anywhere in Rochester. She wanted to dress casually, leave her hair naturally wavy, and go to the local bar for some beer. It helped that the bar was conveniently within walking distance. She dried off her hands and placed the dish towel over the clean dishes.

Before Kevin went into his house, Kate was out on her porch and called across the lawn, "You want some cinnamon bread?"

"Don't tell me you're baking on your birthday?" Kevin asked, laughing at her.

"They wouldn't let me work, so I had some spare time," Kate said, walking over to Kevin with a loaf of bread already in her hands. "It's still warm. You're not gluten-free, are you?"

He looked at her with an *are-you-kidding?* look as he accepted the bread. "Well, thank you, neighbor."

"You're welcome, neighbor. Take this as a thank you for the amazing birthday present," she said.

"Well, I should put lights on your porch more often then," he said, smirking. There was something about his eyes that were so kind, the way they looked at her as though she was unquestionably precious.

Not wanting the conversation to end, Kate added, "We're going down to the bar at six if you want to come. Amy will be there."

"I'm not sure. I'm a mess, and I was going to keep unpacking the boxes that are collecting dust in the garage."

"Alright then. Have a good night," she said, wishing she had gotten a different answer. She made her way back home, her teal summer dress catching the breeze as she turned away from him, creating its own form of art around her body. Art he could not look away from.

"You too. Happy birthday, Kate," he said.

THE BAR WAS busy for a Thursday night. The downtown parking area was nearly full, and music was blaring. Kate walked inside and saw Amy sitting at a high-top table in the corner. Unexpectedly, everyone in the bar turned and yelled, "Happy Birthday!" to Kate.

She froze and ducked a little, frightened from the

sudden surprise. "What the hell!" she yelled over to Amy. All Amy could do was shrug. The bar was filled with regulars from Julie's and friends of Kate's. Nancy and Ashley were there too. She was immediately welcomed to the bar and handed a beer with olives before she could even consider what she wanted to drink. Kate was more introverted than not. She preferred to be in small-gathering situations, if not alone, with her paint and canvases, but she also handled large crowds with ease.

After greeting everyone, she sat with Amy and ordered an appetizer. Kate was glowing. She felt loved, which was a nice change for the rollercoaster of emotions she had been on over the last week.

Cheese curds, boneless buffalo wings, and a pile of French fries later, Kate was ready for another drink. Zan joined after her twelfth suspect interview of the day. She didn't want to ruin Kate's birthday, so she avoided all work talk and kept the information from the case to herself. The day was not about the murderer or the progress they were making. It was about Kate.

The waitress came by with a shot of tequila, lime, and salt. "I didn't order this," Kate said innocently to the waitress.

"Yeah, the guy at the bar did," she replied, pointing to the man at the bar in light jeans, a black button-up long sleeve shirt with the sleeves rolled up to his forearms, and neon orange shoes.

Kevin.

Kate instantly blushed and smiled, waving for him to come over to their table. "You guys, it's Kevin."

"Ooohhh!" Zan and Amy teased her simultaneously.

"You know it's a weeknight, right!?" Kate said to Kevin.

He brought his shot of tequila and lime he planned to do

with her from afar. "But it's only your birthday once this year," he replied without hesitation. "Hey, Amy!"

"Kevin! Long time no see. How are you?" Amy said, hugging him tightly.

"Great. You must have heard that I'm Kate's new neighbor?" Kevin responded.

"Sure did. Keep an eye on her for us, okay?" Amy said.

"Of course," Kevin said, smiling at Kate.

"Well, what the hell are you waiting for?" Zan asked, motioning to the shots of tequila.

Kate and Kevin raised their shots in the air as a sign of cheers.

"Happy birthday!" the table yelled.

Kate lifted her left hand to her mouth, licking the back of her hand with her eyes on Kevin, his eyes on her. It was the slowest pre-salt hand lick Zan and Amy had ever seen. They sprinkled salt on their freshly licked skin, clinked their shots together, and downed the shots of tequila. They finished with the lime while the liquor, or was it Kevin's gaze, warmed Kate from the inside.

"Yeah, Sampson!" Zan yelled, clapping her hands as Amy whistled and cheered along.

"Thanks, neighbor," she quietly said to Kevin. They were in their own world, staring at each other as everyone around them yelled and cheered, clapping to Kate's first birthday shot of the night.

They were laughing and having a great time watching a tipsy couple attempt to dance when a server delivered the second round of shots. This time, it was enough for all four of them. They toasted to Kate, savoring the butterscotch flavor as they drank. She was blissfully happy.

But what Kate didn't know was that Brian was watching at the far end of the bar.

25

SATURDAY, APRIL 24, 2021

7:00 p.m.

Nate had been living in a tent city and on the streets for twenty-five years now. Untreated PTSD, depression, and anxiety worsened as Nate grew up with Ross, Kya, and the others in tent city. He became difficult to raise and difficult to associate with as his untreated mental health ailments grew intense. As time passed, one thought consumed his mind. He wanted to get back at Chuck for what he did to him because of how his life turned out. He wanted him to feel the pain he caused physically, emotionally, and mentally. Chuck needed to pay for all the harm he inflicted on his mother and the drugs he kept her hooked on. He wanted to kill Chuck. But first, he'd make him suffer.

Nate always knew Chuck had three daughters, but Nate had never met them. As the years passed, Nate's darkness grew. It didn't matter to Nate that Chuck didn't raise his three daughters. It didn't matter that they were nothing like Chuck. All that mattered was the fact that they were Chuck's blood, so they contained evil, just like him.

. . .

A MONTH WENT BY, and Nate had been watching her, figuring out who she was. Nate heard Chuck curse her adoptive fathers. He remembered the cruel and sick names he called the men who took in his daughter when he didn't want her. The one he now watched from his car was the daughter who had been hooked on drugs when she was born, Amber.

Nate finally found her, one of the daughters of the man he'd been trying for years to get out of his mind. But instead of feeling bad for her and the awful biological father she didn't know she had, he felt nothing but motivation to hurt. In her face he saw the eyes of the man who caused him so much pain.

On the fifth night of watching Amber from afar, he devised a plan to get into her home through the garage service door, the door she notoriously forgot to lock. He took advantage of his discovery one night and made his way into her home, controlling her with his taller, larger frame and, of course, a large knife he'd gotten from her knife block.

The mask over his face kept her from seeing enough to identify him. All she saw were his eyes, but they were eyes she would never forget. Amber was sure she would die that night, but she was left in her bed as a bloody, beaten mess when he was done with her. As soon as she could, she found her smartwatch and called 911. He'd taken her phone, thinking it was her only way to call the police. He didn't know any better. As someone who grew up in a tent city, he just recently acclimated to the real world. He was living in the home of a man who had been arrested and he was using his clothes, eating his food, and slowly stealing his identity.

That will hurt him, Nate thought to himself, satisfied with his work upon leaving Amber's house. *But he needs to suffer more,* he decided. And that is when he started tracking Stacie.

AFTER HE LEFT Stacie's house, he still had the knife he'd taken from Amber's home. Stacie's blood was on his shirt, where her wounded hand pushed him away. His desire for adrenaline was increasing with every crime. He stayed close, and in the morning, when her husband and son came home, he watched from across the street as police arrived, feeling satisfied that he tied up the loose end by killing her rather than letting her live like he did with Amber.

Nate felt no remorse. He felt no pity for her, no sympathy, no regret. He felt accomplished. Empowered. And now it was time to find the first sister, the oldest. Chuck's firstborn. The first family Chuck had was his happiest family. It was the beginning of a life with the love of his life, but it took a turn when the child he didn't want in the first place was born.

Wise enough to adjust to social norms, Nate fit into society reasonably well. He had nothing from his past—no childhood photos, birth certificate, or biological family. He had Ross and Kya, but their community was not where Nate wanted to spend the rest of his life. He needed more, evidenced by the trouble he caused with the others who lived in their community.

The first incident was months after Nate met Ross and Kya. They found one of the stray cats living in the area dead in the woods. Kya had found her; it was the white cat she had named Snow. But Kya wasn't just upset because Snow was found dead. She was upset because she did not die of natural causes. The deformed shape of her head was her first clue, followed by the nearby rocks painted with blood.

Of course, no one suspected Nate right away, but when blood was found on his shorts, Ross questioned him. "Son, did you kill Snow?" he asked.

"Yes," he admitted. He didn't realize what he did would hurt Kya so much until he and Ross went on a long walk through the woods. Ross explained what he did was wrong, resulting in Nate opening up to him even more about having to live with Chuck.

Animals disappeared now and again since Snow's death, but instead of leaving them in plain sight, Nate hid them, buried them, or took them far enough out into the woods where they wouldn't be found. It felt like an experiment to him and provided him with gratification to hurt something smaller than himself. It put Nate in control. Kya knew what happened and remained suspicious of Nate despite her love for him and the torture he endured before finding his way to Winona. But rather than hurting him in return, yelling at him, and banning him, they showed him love, hoping to teach him the right way to treat people and animals.

Unfortunately, despite years of trying, incidents kept happening, and eventually, they subtly asked Nate to leave the tent city.

Ross had delivered the news to Nate. Kya couldn't bear to tell him. She loved Nate too much to break his heart, but she had grown more afraid of Nate as he aged.

THE SAME DAY Stacie's body was found, Nate started the hunt for the first-born sister. He had more determination than ever as the vivid nightmares came back to Nate full force.

The more life he hurt, the more satisfied he was, yet his PTSD worsened, fueling his rage.

After tracking down the first daughter's hometown, he finally found her. He stood in the street looking through the window, and there she was. Kate Sampson.

26

FRIDAY, JULY 2, 2021

12:59 a.m.

"I am not!" Kate exclaimed, attempting to not slur as she failed to walk in a straight line. Zan and Amy accused her of being drunk. They were feeling full themselves and got a ride home from a sober friend at Kate's party. Kate promised she'd be fine walking home with Kevin. "He knows where I live, you guys, okay?"

"Don't worry, Amy, I'll take care of her. I'll at least make sure she makes it in the house," Kevin said.

Amy smiled and hugged him tight, saying, "I'm so sorry about your brother, Kevin. It was so good to see you!"

Kate turned to Kevin and pointed at his nose, and said, "You! You are drunk. You and those shoes."

"What about my shoes?" Kevin asked.

"They saved you last night. I could have shot you, you know. I was ready. Locked and loaded. Those orange shoes saved you," Kate said, acting as though the shoes pulled him out of a burning building.

"Ah. Well, thank you, shoes," he said, looking down at

his feet. This made Kate laugh, nearly tripping over herself. Kevin caught her like a damsel in distress. He looked at her, smiled, then helped her find her balance. She stopped laughing and looked at him with a serious expression on her face like she had an epiphany. It was yet another gesture that made her realize he was a genuine guy. He stared back, waiting for her to say something or to do something.

"Thank you," she whispered. With these words, he let go. He stepped away, and they kept walking toward home.

"You're welcome. That's what neighbors are for!" Kevin joked, lightening the mood.

The vibrant glow from Kate's porch and the dim glow from Kevin's were welcoming as they walked up Kate's sidewalk.

"You good?" Kevin asked, pretending to be too cool to care too much.

"Water. Advil. Bed. Yes?" Kate asked, sounding a bit more sober than she had before. She unlocked her front door, not realizing she hadn't set the alarm before going to the bar.

"Sounds like a good plan."

"How about some help up the stairs?" Kate asked, referring to the stairs that led to her bedroom.

"Alright," he said hesitantly. He couldn't leave her hanging. He also didn't want to be blamed if she woke up at the bottom of her steps in the morning.

They went to the kitchen, where Kate got what she needed for bed. Kevin grabbed a glass of water for himself as he waited for her to take two Advil. She set down her glass and headed toward her stairs. The two glasses of water Kate had at the bar before leaving were clearing her system. She was still feeling tipsy but far better than she'd been feeling an hour prior.

Kevin followed a couple of steps behind, making sure she kept her balance.

Kate went into her room and said, "Tuck me in, okay?" She didn't wait for an answer but went into her walk-in closet to change. Instead of grabbing her ratty old bedtime t-shirt, she picked her cream-colored silk nightgown.

KEVIN HEARD her dress hit the floor and the clink of a clothes hanger as she grabbed her nightgown. He was speechless when she emerged from her closet. The night-gown accentuated how tan she was, but even more, how beautiful she was. He wanted so badly to scoop her up in his arms and kiss her passionately. It was the kiss he'd been longing to give her since they met. But he didn't. Though, he couldn't help but notice no bra or underwear lines showed through the silk. *She has nothing underneath*, he thought, envisioning all the possible ways that night, or morning could end. He wanted to hold her in his arms and kiss her like she was the only woman on Earth, then slide his hand up her thigh to her waist, knowing there was nothing under-neath to stop him. He wanted to kiss her neck, her collar-bone, and her chest, then pull her silk nightgown down over her shoulders, kissing each side gently as though she were made of glass. He imagined how she would sound breathing into him, moving her body as an invitation to continue. He was aware of his body, clearly turned on yet trying to hold back his arousal.

"Hello?" Kate asked, giggling, snapping him back to real-ity. "I thought I lost you for a minute there. Where did you go?"

"I was zoning out, sorry. Wow," Kevin said, not being able to help himself but knowing he needed to play the friend role tonight. She was in no shape to consent to that. Kate's nightgown slid up as she lifted her knee onto her queen-sized bed to crawl in. He saw the top of her thigh, wanting to savor every inch of her.

She relaxed, got comfortable, and looked at him with inviting eyes, not ready to say goodnight. "This has been one of the best birthdays I've ever had," she said, smiling.

Her chest rose and fell as she breathed, and with every ounce of decency he had, Kevin smiled, pulled the comforter over her, and replied, "I'm so glad." Her eyes looked up at him, and her lips parted. She was breathing deep, then gently bit her lower lip, seeming to want him just as much as he wanted her.

Kevin leaned into her, only inches apart now, and ran his right hand through the hair around her face. "Sweet dreams, Kate."

"Goodnight, Kevin. Thank you," Kate said.

Kevin made his way down the stairs slowly, with his heart and body regretting not asking if he could kiss her, though he knew he did the right thing. Mostly, he was happy he went to her party.

He locked her front doorknob and closed the door behind him, not able to put away his smile. He headed over to his house and went inside. Kevin closed his front door behind him, not knowing someone had been watching from the bushes of the house across the street.

THE SUN HAD WOKEN Kate earlier in the day, but her headache put her right back to sleep. She never "went out" anymore, so she didn't feel bad for sleeping in until 10:00 a.m., knowing Nancy was running the store. When it was 10:30 a.m., she got up. Thankfully, she felt much better by this time. The room spinning was gone, and all she could think about was eating something filling and greasy—comfort food. *A birthday celebration can last two days*, she thought to herself, meandering downstairs in her robe.

She put on a podcast and listened to another episode in which the two female comedians mention how often murderers are found to have had a previous head injury, like a severe concussion. She sat on her porch enjoying the morning air, birds chirping, reminiscing in her mind about how amazing of a night she had with such amazing company. She couldn't help but wonder what would have happened if she'd been sober. She noticed a difference between Kevin and Brian. Kevin could handle his alcohol, easily setting himself a limit, knowing when he needed to stop.

The to-do list in Kate's head was eating at her, so she decided it was time to run errands. She was going to put up new shelves in Julie's. Her hair went into a low bun with short wispy pieces that weren't long enough to pull back, falling near her face. She put on a touch of makeup and made her way downstairs to the front door, heading to her car she rarely used. So much of what she needed was within walking distance of downtown Dover, so the car often sat collecting dust. She would have to go to Rochester, thirty minutes away, to get shelving. As she passed the new lights on her porch, she didn't notice the white rose intertwined in them, blending in with the white lilies.

27

SATURDAY, JULY 3, 2021

4:00 p.m.

July third was Dover's big holiday celebration. While bigger cities and towns had their fireworks on the Fourth of July, Dover celebrated on the third with a show just as spectacular as the surrounding cities. Church ladies were serving hot dogs and chips at the city park, and right across the street, there were free root beer floats at the town fire station. It was one of the few days of the year the entire town came downtown to celebrate. The other big event was in August for Dover Days when the city would hire a live band. People walked downtown and drove their cars, but most of them went on their side-by-sides. No one came down in tractors, though, a tradition local high school students kept alive on the last day of school.

Kate had the store open until noon, a holiday tradition, just long enough for everyone to come to buy their last-minute holiday items before the parties started. She sold out of firecrackers, red solo cups, and sunscreen.

It was seventy-eight degrees when she closed the store

for the day. The high was going to get to eighty-eight, but surely it would feel hotter with the blazing sun and humidity. Kate walked home for lunch and freshened up to go back downtown for the celebration.

Before heading there, she walked over to Kevin's and knocked on his door. He answered wearing only charcoal-colored shorts, no shirt, and no neon orange shoes. She stood there staring, mesmerized by his defined chest and abdominal muscles until he said, "Hey, Kate."

"Hi," she replied, suddenly feeling nervous, nearly forgetting why she went to his house.

"You looked lost there for a minute. Where did you go?" he asked, teasing.

Kate laughed, feeling less anxious with his laid-back demeanor. "I zoned out for a second there. I'm going to head downtown in a little bit. Want to join me?"

"I'm finishing up a project, but how about I freshen up and come over when I'm ready?" he suggested.

"Of course. See ya in a bit," she said, departing back to her house.

THIRTY MINUTES LATER, they were walking to the fire station. Zan would be serving root beer floats, so Kate knew exactly where to find her and Amy. Ashley was there too, chatting with another local. Kevin and Kate got root beer floats, and walked around, checking out the local art on display, jewelry for sale, and chatting with friends along the way. Kevin didn't know many people since he wasn't from Dover, but Kate happily introduced him as her friend and neighbor.

Kate made her way to Ashley, who was heading away from downtown. "Where are you off to?" Kate asked.

"Just heading home," she replied. It was short and sweet. She didn't want to go into detail.

"No Alex?"

"Nope. No big deal, I need the exercise anyway," she said.

"Stop, I'll take you home," Kate offered.

Ashley turned around, stopping in her tracks as though she was giving her decision a second thought. "Well, maybe I'll just stay for a while longer. I don't have any reason to leave. I was just lonely and have already talked to damn near everyone here."

"Hang out with us," Kate said, referring to her and Kevin, who was over at the fire station talking to Zan again. As Kate turned to look at him, she noticed he was talking to someone else. When he turned toward Kate and waved, she suddenly recognized who Kevin was talking to.

It was Brian.

"Hey, Kate. I was just meeting your neighbor. Seems like a pretty nice guy," Brian said.

Kevin didn't know what to say but came up with, "The first time I met Kate was after she fell on her ass trying to fix a light bulb on her porch," he said, and they all laughed. But Kate's laugh was a nervous laugh, high pitch and hesitant.

"I'll let you guys get back to it. I just thought since I am new in town, I'd come down and meet some locals," Brian explained. "Nice to meet you, Kevin."

"Nice to meet you too," Kevin responded. They shook hands, and Brian went on his way, his gaze lingering at Kevin for a heartbeat too long.

"Is it just me, or was that weird?" Kate asked.

"That was weird. Come on, let's go get a drink," Ashley suggested. They walked across the block to the bar, where they were serving margaritas on the patio. It was a hot but memorable afternoon for Kate. One she wouldn't forget.

AS THE SUN SET, Kate led Ashley, Kevin, Amy, and Zan into her store. "You really want to shop at this hour?" Kevin asked, teasing yet confused.

"No, no. You'll see," Kate replied. They went through the back room and through a door that had stairs leading to the roof of Julie's—a perfect place to sit for fireworks.

Ashley came up last, bringing a cooler of beer. "Why does the small girl have to carry the cooler? This thing is damn near heavier than I am!" Ashley complained.

They found seats on the rooftop and chatted until the first firework went off. There was always a big bang first. It was a sign the fireworks would start soon. Two beers, thirty minutes of fireworks, and an hour of chatting later, they stood to head back downstairs. This time, Kevin carried the cooler.

"Sure, now he takes it. Now that it's empty!" Ashley complained.

"Anything I can do to help," Kevin replied, winking at her. Zan and Amy drove Ashley home as Kevin and Kate walked. This time, Kate was not drunk, nor was Kevin. The margaritas from earlier had passed through their systems a long time ago, and two beers did nearly nothing for them. When they reached Kate's front porch, they stood on the top step, still not noticing the white rose that looped into the lights beside them.

"I'm beat," Kate said. Her shoulders were darkened from the sun, and there was a pink area where she missed putting sunscreen. Kevin put his hand on her shoulder, pointing out the pink spot, and she laughed. "I was just trying to be colorful, okay?"

Kate made humor from the nerves she felt, but his hand on her shoulder gave her warm chills throughout her body. She stared at him, biting her lower lip, leaning into him just a touch, but close enough to invite him to lean in too. His hand slid from her shoulder to her neck, and he gently pulled her close. He kissed her softly but passionately and felt her arms slide around his waist, pulling him in closer. Her right hand moved up to his chest, and she continued to kiss him, falling deeper into a state of passion.

When the moment ended, their foreheads were together, and they breathed deep, both clearly wanting more but knowing it would have been moving fast. He pulled her in for one more kiss and said, "Goodnight, neighbor."

"Sleep well, neighbor," she replied.

11:30 P.M. is what the clock showed when she finally crawled into bed. She spent a while staring at the ceiling, smiling because of the wonderful evening she had. There was a party on the next block, but this didn't bother her. Even when they kept lighting fireworks late into the night, she was too happy to care. She fell asleep to the sound of fireworks, thinking nothing of the noises she heard.

28

3:05 a.m.

The sound of the fireworks had stopped, but something else woke her up. Kate grabbed her phone and checked for notifications. There were none. No indication someone was near her front door, no alarms going off, no warnings. Wide awake, she didn't move. Thunder rolled, and rain fell on the steel roof. Nerves coursed through her body as she had flashbacks from her childhood, feeling her heart beat hard in her chest wall. *He's not here. He's not here,* she kept telling herself, not pinpointing whether she was referring to her childhood rapist or the modern-day murderer.

Rain was falling hard, making it challenging to hear anything else happening in her house. But she heard a new noise now, a quiet clattering of something downstairs. Then, the floorboard on her stairs creaked. Kate grabbed her gun from under the pillow where she left it locked and loaded and pointed it at her bedroom door.

. . .

FROM THE TOP of the stairs, he was dripping wet from the rain. His hunting mask, hiding his identity, was soaked, but he hardly noticed. He only had one thing on his mind. He peered through her bedroom door from the hallway's darkness and saw her sitting up in bed. She was holding something. But what?

Recapping the last few opportunities he had to enter her home, he knew this would be his last chance. He went for it.

The bedroom door flew open after he kicked it with his boot. He ran toward Kate with his large knife from Amber's house, smashing her into her headboard as his knife sliced her left arm. The gun she had in her hand went off, but she wasn't ready enough to take proper aim. The shot made him pause with pain and surprise, but he did not fall. Not knowing where she shot him, she thrust him off, accidentally throwing the gun too. *Run. She had to run.* She bolted out of her room and down the stairs as fast as she could.

The bullet had gone into his abdomen, but he kept going, his rage and adrenaline dulling the pain. He was like a semi-truck on a mission, and nothing could stop him until she was eradicated. He got up and rushed after her, missing the gun next to him on the floor. He had to finish this, finish her. He was only a couple of seconds behind.

KATE MADE it to her hiding place before he got to the bottom of the steps. The closet under the stairs was small and full of luggage and miscellaneous bags. She hid between them, trying to control her breathing. *Fuck, I should have put a panic button in here,* she thought, suddenly thinking of all the ways she should have been better protected. She did not know how he got in, but at the moment, her mind was focused on survival. She devised a plan to get out.

The bottom step creaked as he put his weight on it. She heard him round the corner, assuming he would wander the house until he found her. His breathing was loud enough for her to hear, likely from pain from the gunshot wound. She stopped hearing him after a minute and wondered what he was doing.

Suddenly, her front door opened and shut as though he had left. She sighed quietly with relief and stayed in the closet for a few more minutes to be sure he was gone. She heard nothing.

Kate crept out of the storage closet and looked around the room, seeing nothing, hearing nothing, smelling nothing. She inched her way to the kitchen and tiptoed backward, oblivious to the trail of blood she was leaving from her arm. Five more steps backward, and she would be at the back patio door where she could run for help.

A floorboard near her dining room creaked. Through the rain, she still recognized the sound. It was a board just around the kitchen corner, and she sensed a sudden rush of impending doom in the pit of her stomach. She ran to the patio door as he darted around the corner toward her. He was too quick. He grabbed her and pulled her back toward him. Her fight was strong, and he was barely holding on when he punched her hard on her left cheek, knocking her to the floor. He straddled Kate now, putting his hands around her neck, pinning her to the ground. She was unable to breathe, just as Stacie couldn't in her bathtub. He had to fight to keep her down, but soon her fight weakened, and she was growing dizzy.

As her body grew tired, her mother's face appeared in her mind. *Hold on, my love,* Julie said to her. *Hold on.*

There was a sudden loud noise, the sound of metal hitting a skull. A moment later, there was a thud when his body landed on the ground next to Kate. She gasped for air and coughed, rolling away from the man who lay on the floor next to her. The bat had hit the left side of his head, and blood pooled around him as he lay only a couple of feet away from Kate. He was still breathing. His blade was next to his unmoving body, so Kate quickly grabbed it and pointed it at him once she caught her breath. She turned her head to view the dark figure with the bat on the other side of her kitchen. He was wearing a dark sweater and jeans, but she couldn't see his face.

She stood, reached for the light switch and flipped it on.

29

SUNDAY, JULY 4, 2021

3:35 a.m.

The man stood before Kate with her bat from her front entryway in his right hand. He raised his left hand and pulled down the drenched hood that covered his head to reveal himself. Brian's eyes quickly met Kate's.

"Brian?" she asked, shaking with fear and confusion. But who was the masked man who lay at her feet?

Brian pulled out his cell phone and dialed 911 as Kate sat on the floor holding her arms to her chest. Brian walked over to Kate, crouched down, and put an arm around her shoulder, trying to comfort her as he said, "We need police and medical to 555 Maple Street in Dover. There's been a break-in, and the intruder received a baseball bat to the head. He's currently not moving but appears to be breathing."

Who?

"Do you know the suspect, sir?" dispatch asked Brian.

"His name is Nathan Grey," he said, "but he's been going by an alias, Alex."

She gasped. *What?* Kate gazed down at the man on the floor, recognizing the shaggy blonde hair sticking out from the bottom of his mask. She recognized his dirty clothes even though he looked like a jock. She recognized Alex.

POLICE ARRIVED MINUTES LATER. Brian asked Kate if she was okay and if he hurt her. The sirens were muted through the sound of the storm. Lights were blazing as law enforcement parked their cars and ran inside. Within seconds, they had invaded Kate's kitchen.

Brian kicked the bat away from himself and raised his hands as though he was a suspect before saying, "Brian Thompson, private investigator. This man has been going by the name of Alex, but his real name is Nathan Grey. His mom called him Nate. He's been missing since 1996." A deputy kneeled on the floor, assessing Nate just after he handcuffed him. Nate was still not moving, but he was breathing. The pool of blood around his head stopped growing, and the deputy motioned for the paramedics to come into the kitchen.

"Kate!" Kevin entered the doorway of the kitchen, soaking wet. "Kate! Oh my God, are you okay? Are you hurt?" He ran over to her, knelt down and hugged her tight as Brian stepped away.

"I'm okay," she replied. "What is going on?" she finally asked Brian, bewildered.

"Long story, we can talk about more details later," Brian replied. "I've been looking for Nathan, and we had an inkling he'd be somewhere close to where you were."

Kate stood with the help of Kevin. She was stunned and could hardly process what Brian was saying.

"We?" Kate asked.

Brian didn't react to Kevin's closeness with Kate. Instead he professionally stated, "Nathan Gray has been missing since 1996. Natalie, his mom, has been looking for him for years. She recently hired me to track him down. Something in the back of her mind was throwing up a red flag about the safety of Kate."

Kate looked at Brian and anxiously asked, "Why?"

"After Amber's rape and Stacie's murder." He stopped and took a breath, "Kate, Natalie knew Amber and Stacie were the victims of those crimes through the news and small-town gossip. But she also knew they were related; she connected the dots. Kate, they are your half-sisters."

Shock consumed her. Goosebumps took over her skin, she felt cold, pale, and nauseous. The air grew thick, and she felt like she couldn't breathe. Kevin pulled Kate in close to him, watching her grow ill before his eyes.

"What the hell are you talking about?" Kate demanded.

"Kate, when Nathan Grey ran away in 1996, it was because he was being raped by his mother's boyfriend, Chuck. Natalie found a journal of Nate's a year after he'd gone missing. That's where she found out that he was being abused by Chuck. She thought it would be such a long shot that Nate was the criminal in this case. Hell, she hardly believed he was even still alive. But now, it's apparent Nate has returned to hurt Chuck in any way he could, and that was to hurt his three daughters. Natalie wanted to find her son. But she also wanted to protect you," Brian explained. "Kate, you're the first sister. Chuck had you, then Amber, then Stacie."

There was a moment of silence until Kate looked up to ask, "So this guy isn't Alex?"

"No. But I do think we need to get ahold of Ashley as soon as we can," Brian added.

Ashley! Kate thought.

An ambulance crew was on the ground by Nate with a stretcher as other paramedics approached Kate to assess her. She was resistant because she wanted to get to Ashley's house as soon as she could. But after looking at the blood pooling on the floor from the gash in her arm, she complied. They quickly strapped a bandage on her arm before they loaded Nate onto the stretcher. He was in rough shape, floating in and out of consciousness.

Kate, Kevin, and Brian got into Brian's car as the EMT loaded Nate into the ambulance. They sped away toward Ashley's house, knowing Nate would be going to the local emergency room for immediate medical care. From there, police would place him in custody as soon as he was deemed healthy enough.

30

SUNDAY, JULY 4, 2021

    4:15 a.m.

Making it to Ashley's house in record time, Brian, Kate, and Kevin ran through the darkness to Ashley's door as two deputies followed close behind. "Ashley! Ashley!" Kate yelled, pounding on her door.

Brian stepped beside Kate and said, "Allow me." He positioned her away from the door, lifted his right foot, and smashed the door in, opening it with a force that put a hole in her wall from the door handle.

For a moment, none of them could move; it was an awful scene. Her house was destroyed. There was a broken coffee table and lamp in the living room, the kitchen table turned on its side along with two chairs, and a trail of blood from her dining room to her kitchen. Where the trail ended was a bloody, broken, beaten mess. She was barely recognizable. It was Ashley.

Kate ran to her and screamed, "Ashley! Someone help! Ashley!" Unable to calm herself enough to see if she was still alive, she picked up Ashley's head and hugged it tightly, crying hysterically while rocking back and forth.

"Uhhh," the noise came from Ashley.

"Ashley! It's me. Wake up, please. I'm right here. I'm here," Kate said. "Open your eyes, honey, please? Hang on, okay? Paramedics are coming."

A second ambulance crew arrived and ran into the house with their bags and a stretcher. Zan and Douglas were right behind, both in street clothes since they weren't on duty.

Paramedics got on the ground next to Ashley as Kevin moved to Kate, putting his hands on her shoulders. "Kate, let's let them work," he said, encouraging her to step back.

The crew surrounded Ashley, hastening to place a blood pressure cuff to check her vital signs. They set a cervical collar around her neck and rolled her onto a backboard to transfer her to the stretcher. They lifted the stretcher as one of the medics was setting an IV and they quickly made their way out of the house and to the ambulance, Kate following close behind. She turned around and saw Kevin and Brian standing outside of the house looking at her.

Brian said, "Go. I'll bring Kevin. Go," encouraging her to stay with Ashley.

"SHE HAS SWELLING in her brain, three broken ribs, a broken arm and wrist, a cracked cheekbone along with multiple other scratches and bruises," Kate explained to Brian, Kevin, Zan, and Douglas. "I should have known. I should have known," she cried, blaming herself for what happened.

Kevin pulled her into his chest, hugging her tight. "No one knew, Kate," he said, running a hand through her hair.

"But she came in with a black eye last week. She said she

fell into her counter. I don't know why I believed her. I'm so stupid! And then her phone. He must have broken her phone because she would never leave it on the top of the car. Her phone is attached to her at all times. I knew this," Kate continued. They tried to ease her guilt, but the weight of it consumed her.

Later, Amy brought doughnuts from the local bakery to the hospital, where everyone was waiting anxiously. Kate couldn't eat; her mind was racing, and she kept putting off being examined by the ER doctors. "That can wait," she demanded. "I need to be here for her right now."

She turned to Brian to shift the conversation, hoping he'd answer the endless questions she had racing through her mind. "You said Natalie wanted to protect me. Why?"

"She didn't know who you were or where you were. She just knew there was a *you* and that you were in danger," Brian explained. "This is what brought me to town, Kate. I'm not a business guy, but I was here for a job, to find you and Nate."

Kate nodded, trying to process. Brian started walking down the hallway toward the vending machine, and she followed.

Brian turned to say, "I shouldn't have gotten involved with you, Kate. I'm so sorry."

She looked up at him not saying anything, so he continued, "You're just so beautiful." He looked into her eyes, then looked away with shame before saying, "I have a drinking problem. I know this. Some of the jobs I've worked on have been extremely traumatic, but that is no excuse. After meeting you, Kate, I'm looking to get help. When I asked you on a date, that was me. Not the investigator side of me." His glazed eyes peered back into hers. She felt his sincerity.

"I wasn't ready for you, though, and you're with someone

who looks at you like nothing else in the world matters. I've seen it. You deserve that, Kate," Brian explained.

"I had no idea," Kate said quietly.

"I didn't want you to figure it out," Brian explained. "I'm so sorry."

"I understand," she said with a small nod. To his surprise she said, "Friends?"

He smiled at her, "Friends."

They walked back to the waiting area, where everyone else sat. "Why the white rose petals?" Zan asked Brian.

"Natalie said white roses were the only flowers Chuck gave her. Nate loved them, I guess. But they also reminded him of evil, so it seems. She got white roses when she and Nate returned home from the hospital when he was a kid. She told me that she planned to leave him when Nate got out of the hospital, but he manipulated her into staying with him. Chuck had given Nate such a severe concussion that he was hospitalized for days. Who knew something so beautiful could represent something so heinous," Brian replied.

The on-call neurosurgeon came out of the double doors leading to Ashley's ICU bed. He gently approached everyone and announced, "She's in a medically induced coma until the swelling of her brain comes down. She's stable for now, but we'll have to reassess when we bring her out of the coma."

Cold tears flooded Kate's face. She didn't know what to say or do. "I can call you when we plan to wake her up," the doctor said.

"Please do," Kate replied, nodding her head, knowing there was nothing more they could do at the hospital. Despite visiting hours being over, they allowed Kate to go into her ICU room for a minute. Ashley had listed Kate as her emergency contact on her medical forms. Though she was not much younger, Ashley was like a little sister to Kate.

Kate cautiously approached Ashley's ICU bed as the nurse told her, "She may hear you." Kate had to pause to gain her composure before she approached the bed and held Ashley's hand.

"I'm so sorry, Ashley. I'm so sorry. I should have known. This is all my fault," she said, trying to hide the fact that she was crying. Kate leaned down to kiss her on the cheek and combed her fingers through her silky blonde hair, and said, "I love you. I'm right here, okay? I love you."

31

2:35 p.m.

The trial lasted four days. Tensions were high as the jury deliberated. Two hours later, they'd reached a verdict. Nate Grey sat next to his appointed defense attorney as the jury members walked in. He still had shaggy blonde hair, but now he had ratty facial hair that gave him a more unkempt appearance. Under all of that, Natalie could still see her little boy who carried the bitter expression he had when he left their home in 1996.

The attorneys collaborated with the judge, and she looked at Nate before they proceeded with the verdict. What Nate didn't know was that Chuck was in prison as well. He'd beaten his most recent girlfriend in a drunken rage. After, he left her in a bloody heap on the floor of her bedroom. Her phone was on the nightstand, only four feet away. It took everything she had to get to it.

Within six minutes, deputies and an ambulance arrived at their house. When they entered, deputies read Chuck the Miranda rights and cuffed him while the medics found her bedroom according to the directions the dispatcher had received upon her call. She was nearly unconscious on the floor when she was found, and they saw her bruised eyes swollen shut. She had a fat and bloody lip with a front tooth missing and multiple areas of redness that would soon turn to bruises. What they'd find in the ER would be broken ribs and a swollen spleen that had thankfully stopped internally bleeding on its own. Nearly killing his girlfriend landed Chuck in prison, and the paraphernalia found in the home added to the number of felonies he was charged with. At the time of Nate's arrest, Chuck had five years left to serve in prison. Natalie knew Chuck was a big reason why Nate left. But despite the terrible things Nate had done, she still wanted to reconnect with her son.

Natalie, Ross, and Kya sat in the courtroom together. They came to see their little boy, who was verbally, physically, and mentally abused. Their little boy, the one who also sustained a significant concussion, had grown up to be a monster, so the evidence showed. What would he have been like if Chuck hadn't lived with Natalie?

In addition to having found Nate in Kate's home, the evidence showed his fingerprints on the glass-cutter he used to cut the window. He'd chosen a living room window and carefully removed the glass so it wouldn't fall in her house and shatter. The hole was just large enough so he could reach his arm in and remove the sensor from her window, keeping the two pieces together so the sensor would not go off. He then reached her lock and unlocked her window. He removed the screen and crawled in.

The fingerprints from Nate matched prints from Amber's home, Stacie's home, and now Kate's. On top of the evidence, Nate had nothing to say about the case. He did not deny that he hurt those women, nor did he confess. He simply said nothing at all.

"WE, the jury, find the defendant guilty," said one of the jurors.

Ross put an arm around Kya, and Natalie sat staring straight ahead. They knew it was coming, but it was still a shock. Kya put a hand on Natalie's back, and finally, she broke down. She cried because the only way she'd get to know her little boy was through a prison telephone and limited visitations, but given the circumstances, she knew that was for the best. She put so much blame on herself for not knowing he'd been abused and for not leaving Chuck when Nate had begged her to.

Natalie became a free spirit after leaving Chuck. It was a new beginning. She had no more children and hardly dated. She spent much of her time trying to track down Nate, to no avail. She finally got a stable job as a receptionist at a law firm in Rochester, and because of the work she'd been doing there, she knew Nate would be in prison for life.

There was no remorse, no anger, no expression on Nate's face after they read the verdict. He simply sat and stared like a soulless body, taking up space in the world. Natalie couldn't help but see the child in him. She saw his shaggy hair and the faint freckles on his face and arms. She saw him sleeping on his bed, curled up in a ball on the night before he left for his first day of school, on the day he didn't come home. It was an image she'd never forget. She was awake in the middle of the night and went to check on him, almost waking him up to tell him she wanted to pack up their things at that very moment and leave. But she didn't.

She didn't want to wake him. Instead, he woke up in the morning, got himself ready, and never came home.

As the deputies escorted Nate out of the room, he glanced at the audience seeing his mother, instantly recognizing her. He stopped and said, "Make sure he knows."

She knew right then he was referring to Chuck and replied quietly, only for herself to hear, "He will, my son. He will."

32

FRIDAY, OCTOBER 1, 2021

12:35 p.m.

Nate sat in an orange jumpsuit across from his mother, who was more beautiful than ever. She filled out since she had become sober. She looked professional, intelligent, and was finally at a healthy weight with thick long, dark hair. Nate hardly recognized her.

Natalie knew Chuck was in the same prison as Nate, but she didn't want to bring it up to him as they likely had yet to cross paths. Instead, she asked with a broken heart, "Where have you been this whole time?"

Words did not come easy for Nate. He looked and felt dead inside as he stared at her. "Safe," he finally replied.

"Oh honey," Natalie replied with sorrow in her eyes. "I'm so sorry, Nate. I'm so, so sorry." Her little boy was finally found, but they were still apart, separated by iron bars and plexiglass. She loved him as much as she always had, knowing he could have had such a different life if she hadn't been so consumed by drugs, alcohol, and Chuck.

"I shouldn't have stayed," she said, wiping her eyes with

the back of her hand. There was no response from the other side of the glass.

Knowing he wouldn't talk much, she made use of their time together and said, "I've been sober, Nate." She told him things that had happened over the years, and as each minute passed, his eyes appeared to liven up.

AFTER A LENGTHY VISIT, Natalie grabbed her purse as she said goodbye to Nate. "I love you, Nate. I will come to see you again." His eyes followed her face as she stood to leave.

"Mom," Nate said.

"Yes, sweetie?" she replied, shocked he was speaking.

"He's here."

"Who?"

"Chuck. He's here."

EPILOGUE

Sunday, December 26, 2021

5:45 p.m.

Kate, Zan, and Amy decorated The Dugout with pink balloons, streamers, and glitter everywhere. Everyone showed up early, and the lights went low just a minute before six o'clock.

The door creaked open, and Ashley stuck her head in, completely confused as to why the place was dark.

The lights flipped on, and the entire bar yelled, "Happy Birthday!" Country music came on, and everyone raised their drinks to toast Ashley for her birthday.

"Don't you guys know I was in a coma earlier this year?" she yelled, laughing. "You're going to make me go back into one!"

"Yeah, yeah. The doctors cleared you. You're fine," Zan said, brushing off her complaint. Ashley was now sporting short blonde hair. She had to go into surgery while she was in the hospital, and they shaved part of her head to get to where they needed to cut. Upon waking up and realizing her hair situation, she told the nurse, "Fuck it. Get me some clippers. You only live once, yeah?"

Later in the night, after a few rounds of beers, a notification came up on Kate's phone, but this time it wasn't a notification from her alarm system. It was a notification of a new episode of her favorite podcast. Much to their surprise, the two-sentence summary included Amber's, Stacie's, Ashley's, and Kate's names. This podcast never interviewed victims and survivors but took news articles, blogs, documentaries, and based-on-true-story films to gather their information for each episode.

They connected Kate's phone to the bar speakers and pressed play. "Georgia. You're going to love this. I mean, I can't believe this story just happened. It's a true crime, rape and murder story, but my favorite part of all is able to talk about the survivors. They're badass women, that's for damn sure. It's the story of the murder of Stacie and the survival of Ashley, Kate, and Amber from southeast Minnesota." Everyone in the bar cheered as though they were at a live show.

The girls weren't ashamed of what had happened to them. Instead, Amber and Kate would continue telling their story, raising awareness, and advocating against sexual assault. They used their experiences to help other survivors get through similar situations. They also educated the public on what survivors go through and how they can help survivors get through their situations. Ashley became an advocate for domestic abuse, speaking in women's shelters and at women's conferences. It was a passion for them, using their experiences of trauma for good. Not only were they helping their community, but they were helping themselves as well.

Amber and Kate met with the help of Brian and Zan. Natalie had brought to light that Kate was the first sister, and they both wanted to meet each other. Everyone met for lunch in the park, and though it was a heartbreaking revelation, the family and their support grew bigger that day. Natalie told Amber and Kate about their father, Chuck. They could hardly believe what they were hearing. Disgusted that their sperm-donor was such a horrendous person; they were still glad to get to know each other. Through the trial and sentencing of Nate, Amber and Kate were each other's key support. And Kevin, of course—Kate's official boyfriend.

"Did Karen say my name last because I'm younger than you?" Amber questioned Kate, referring to the podcast that played over the bar speakers. They laughed and hugged. Kevin leaned into Kate and kissed her on the cheek.

Looking around at her friends, Zan, Amy, Kevin, and Amber, she realized it was the start of their time together as a family. It was the day after Christmas, the anniversary of Julie's death, and a new beginning with new loved ones.

BOOKS BY

DANIELLE LOUISE LEUKAM

Four Pounds of Pressure: A Memoir of Rape, Survival, and Taking Back My Power

Fly Like a Girl: Adventures of Erin and Brad

Made in the USA
Middletown, DE
22 October 2022

13308212R00106